Charlotte Godkin's imagination and spiritual knowledge are introduced in this book. Charlotte thinks very deeply about religion and out-of-body experiences, having experiences that she could not explain.

This book gently takes the reader into spiritual paths that are easier to doubt than try to accept, and yet Charlotte hopes that the curiosity of the reader will keep the pages turning and place a smile on their faces. Premonitions, she can only follow in order to protect animals and human life, in this unpredictable world we all live in. The struggle to understand her own gift and insight!

Katie, my wonderful friend in Norway, and her amazing family.

Simon Hadden, a sincere and wonderful friend, I am fortunate and blessed to know him. My sister and her family.

Christine White, who is such a good friend.

Charlotte Godkin

MISS DAISY WEED'S WHOOPS A DAISY

AUSTIN MACAULEY PUBLISHERS™

LONDON • CAMBRIDGE • NEW YORK • SHARJAH

Ordering Information
Quantity sales: Special discounts are available on quantity purchases by corporations, associations, and others. For details, contact the publisher at the address below.

Publisher's Cataloging-in-Publication data
Godkin, Charlotte
Miss Daisy Weed's Whoops a Daisy

ISBN 9798889106036 (Paperback)
ISBN 9798889106043 (ePub e-book)

Library of Congress Control Number: 2023919190

www.austinmacauley.com/us

First Published 2024
Austin Macauley Publishers LLC
40 Wall Street, 33rd Floor, Suite 3302
New York, NY 10005
USA

mail-usa@austinmacauley.com
+1 (646) 5125767

Dr. Angus & Virginia Armstrong

My amazing publishers, Austin Macauley, so helpful and patient. Thank you.

Table of Contents

Introduction

It had been such a happy time! Sally, Mr. Hill's youngest daughter, had married handsome Johnny Brown. The fairies at the bottom of Mr. Hill's garden had also enjoyed this happy occasion, helping with the donkeys from Hill's Donkey Sanctuary, now Brown's Donkey Sanctuary. All flowers and creatures had wonderful thoughts and memories of Sally and Johnny's wedding.

The two Miss Daisy Weed's flower fairies looked at each other, sad and confused. Why were they feeling sad and not happy as they were just a short time ago? Horace, the friendly garden spider, limped over the wet January grass to where the flower fairies sat on a rock beside a large fir tree. Horace looked so sad.

"What is it, Horace? Are your legs bothering you? Or has your son, Horace two, had more family for your mother to take care of?" The two flower fairies giggled, then realizing they had been a little rude, stopped, and apologized sincerely. "Sorry, Horace, what is wrong?"

"It is Lucy. She has been awake most of the past few nights, in fact, since the wedding night."

"Oh, Horace, how caring you are, is she crying, perhaps missing Sally."

"Nice sweet flower fairies, that were rude to poor Horace, but that is alright." Horace looked down at the ground with a very sad expression. "You see, little Daisy flower fairies, she is writing in her pink book, also she has taken a few photographs of me with her mobile phone, which has me very worried."

"Why on earth should you be worried, Horace, because Lucy takes a few photographs of you, surely you should be more concerned that you are residing on her pink cushion on the chaise in her bedroom!"

"No, no, flower fairies, you are missing the point I am making as usual. Firstly, Lucy likes me to be in her bedroom and secondly, I fear Lucy is going to sell me to the highest bidder."

"Now you have definitely lost us. Can you explain why you would think Lucy is about to sell you?"

"A while ago before Sally met Johnny I was resting after a little bath in Lucy's washbasin, and I heard her talking to Sally." Horace gulped and then continued, his eyes looking very scared. "Lucy said don't worry Sally, I will sell my doll and give you the money for the donkey sanctuary." Horace this time tried a convincing sniff. "She then took a picture of the doll, and wrote something in the pink book, and made a phone call, and when I next went to her bedroom, the doll had gone."

Horace did look worried as he continued, "I heard her talking to Sally a little while later explaining that she had some money from the sale of her doll and that she would look for other things to sell to raise money." Poor sad and frightened Horace gulped. "You see, Daisy flower fairies, I will bring a large price."

The two Daisies patted poor Horace comfortingly on his head, but then could not stop a little giggle. "We somehow think you have got it incorrect, Horace, and we will find out what is in the pink book. In fact, Horace do not worry at all, you have so cheered us up, so to do this for you dear friend is a pleasure, leave it with us, and go and rest, when you wake we will have good news I am sure!"

They flew at speed to Lucy's bedroom window but the window was locked so they decided to peep through the glass. The pink book lay open on Lucy's bed and what caught their eyes shook them from wing to wing. It was a sketch of them, both their wings outstretched and their petals pink-tinged. What could this mean? Were they to be sold and not Horace, after all, they were rather extraordinary and extremely rare.

The Daisy flower fairies were still sitting on the windowsill of Lucy's bedroom when the phone on Lucy's bedside table rang. Lucy, out of breath after her rush upstairs to grab the landline phone before it went to answer phone, reached across the bed and answered, "Hullo, Lucy here. Oh, Sally, it is so good to hear your voice. I have so missed you!" Lucy could hardly take in what she was hearing. "Sally, please calm down and tell me again what I am to do if you cannot return until later."

Sally sat on the bed where Johnny lay, his face white and hollow, dark shadows under his eyes. Sally spoke slowly and cried bitterly. "It's Johnny, Lucy, he is so ill and they are going to take him off the ship to a hospital. I am going with him."

"In fact, the ship doctor thinks it might be food poisoning as other passengers and some crew members are ill. The doctor has said I may have to isolate if they find out it is something else, not sure quite what that means!"

"Please do not worry, Sally. Johnny is a strong man, he will pull through. Meanwhile, dear friend, you need to tell me what I need to do regarding the donkey sanctuary."

"Oh, and Snowdrops has his cough back as he would not go in the barn. I tried everything."

Chapter 1
A Special Kind of Bubble

The weeks turned into months and Johnny Brown's cruise ship, where he worked as a pastry chef, turned into a make-ship hospital. The virus had quickly spread through the ship, and even the fortunate passengers that had managed to escape the deadly virus had to isolate. Rather than risk taking the passengers and sick crew members to a local hospital where the ship had docked, they remained confined to their cabins.

Johnny and Sally had the best cabin on the ship, as they were on their honeymoon, so they were the lucky ones. Sally wheeled Johnny regularly onto their balcony, so as to give him plenty of fresh air and after two weeks of listening to him gasping for air, he began to breathe more steadily. Sally tended to Johnny's needs day and night, but it was professional help she needed.

Twice a day a doctor arrived complete with the ship's doctor and examined Johnny, who appeared to have an untreatable virus. Oxygen was given to Johnny and medication to take down his temperature but the fever continued, but apart from a new vaccine, yet to be discovered, Johnny's life hung in Sally's prayers.

Eventually, Johnny and Sally were moved to a hospital not far from where the ship had docked. It was there with the devoted doctors and nurses, who were willing to risk their own lives, did Johnny make an astonishing recovery. Sally did also catch the virus as her antibodies showed, yet apart from ten days of a headache and constant tiredness, she was fine.

Once Johnny was feeling well enough to return to a normal life, Sally returned her thoughts and worries to Brown's Donkey Sanctuary. Several weeks later, they were flown back to the United Kingdom and arrived back at Sally's father's house. Mr. Hill had constantly telephoned Sally but it was not until his new son-in-law spoke on the phone, did he relax. Judge Arthur, as normal, had been a constant godsend and rock to lean on, giving him positive thoughts through the blackest of days.

As Sally and Johnny, wearing face masks, entered Mr. Hill's house, words were the furthest from each of their lips. Mr. Hill held his daughter in his arms, having believed this moment would never come. With an arm open to place around Johnny, the three stood motionless. It was only when Judge Arthur spoke did the three release their hold and made their way to the sofa.

Judge Arthur did not receive an answer so returned from the kitchen with a mixture of drinks, a glass of milk, a pot of tea, and buttered tea cakes. He placed them on the tea trolley and placed the trolley in front of the sofa, where they could help themselves.

Judge Arthur helped himself to Mr. Hill's whiskey decanter and sat down in the winged armchair to hear in detail what these two young people had experienced over the past months. There was a lot to take in and a lot sounded like a horror movie, however the pandemic, as it was now known, was worldwide.

It was a tired Johnny who changed the subject of the pandemic and asked, "What has been happening to the sanctuary? Are all the donkeys surviving?"

Sally interrupted Johnny as she asked about Snowdrop's cough. Judge Arthur, feeling on top of the world again after his second large scotch, answered that question happily. "Lucy has found a way to get Snowdrops in the barn so his cough has totally gone. Lucy puts Anna, the new donkey, in the barn and Snowdrops—follows, as he is in love with her."

They all laughed, and the mood lightened up with laughter and love. Sally clenched her father's hand and kissed him tenderly on the cheek, saying, "We are in the same bubble!"

Judge Arthur jumped to his feet and held his hand out to the waiting Johnny who had got to his feet, the two men hugged each other. The doorbell rang and as Lucy rushed in and hugged her best friend Sally, the bubble was complete.

Sir Arthur, who always believed in no time like the present, caught the attention of Lucy after the girly chat between Sally and Lucy had its first silence. Lucy, not needing any explanation from Judge Arthur, quickly found the appropriate black book and gold diary in her rather swish pink briefcase. She opened the two books on the date January 11, the day after Johnny and Sally's wedding.

Lucy explained as once the virus had become worldwide, she had started virtual visits to the donkey sanctuary. A large grin appeared across Lucy's face as she emphasized 'Brown's Donkey Sanctuary'. Sally kissed Johnny on the hand as they heard their name mentioned.

"The donkeys birthdays are all written down in this pink and black diary, and the donkeys birthdays that we don't know, I have guessed, so all our donkeys have a special day."

"The people who have adopted our donkeys have first priority to make a virtual visit on that day."

"We do, however, expect them to pay an admittance fee."

"We also have a gift shop online, where items relating to the sanctuary can be purchased."

"Items such as book markers with many of our donkeys pictures on, and rather nice little poems. Aprons with carrot cake recipes, ladies' fur slippers with large donkey ears on. Diaries and pens displaying most of the donkeys' names and pictures of the sanctuary in gold or silver frames. Ladies' lace hankies with initials appropriate and straw hats, oh, and also umbrellas with pictures of the donkey sanctuary, which we felt was a kind of free advertising on a wet day. I have more ideas to add but felt this was enough to start with."

Lucy paused and looked at Sally and added, "I am open to suggestions."

Sally giggled and added, "In that case, Lucy, I suggest we have some hot chocolate and I also suggest that Johnny and I leave shortly, to go to our cottage, and if there is any time left call on our grandparents."

"Then perhaps we could all meet up at some time tomorrow and go over what is needed to be done."

Sally, feeling extremely tired after the long journey and hoping that a good night's sleep would solve that, suggested a meeting at 2 PM the following day. The return to their cozy cottage was the best feeling the couple had felt in such a long time.

As expected, their grandparents had lit a log fire and placed some early spring flowers in a vase. The smell of apple pie greeted them somehow, making the cottage even more homely. They discovered the freshly baked pie on the kitchen table, together with a jug of cream.

They sat side by side on the green newly covered Edwardian sofa and ate the delicious apple pie with cream. Johnny looked at his wife Sally and asked in a quiet voice. "Do you have any regrets, my darling? Our honeymoon turned into a nightmare and I fear it is now a lot of work ahead with the Brown's Donkey Sanctuary."

"No regrets, my darling husband, for if I did not know before how much I loved you, I certainly know now, as I almost lost you."

Lucy was wide awake after having a second cup of hot chocolate and decided to walk back home using the path that ran along the back of the houses. It was a quicker but darker option so she borrowed Mr. Hills torch. As she walked to the bottom of Mr. Hill's garden to the gate to join the path, something strange caught her eye.

At first, Lucy thought it was shadows caused by the full moon, which was throwing an eerie light on the garden. Lucy was not sure she even wanted to know what had first caught her eye, as she already had a list of unexplained things.

However, Lucy's curiosity got the better of her and she returned to the position she had seen strange small shadows in the moonlight. She kneeled down and peered through a gap of bracken, she gasped and quickly turned away for fear she could not breathe if she kept looking at the unbelievable scene.

She rolled over and quietly peeped through the gap once again. This time, she did not turn away but stared almost hypnotized by the incredible vision in front of her eyes. The colors of the wings of the little fairies glistened in the moonlight.

A faint noise appeared to be coming from a fairy that was sitting on top of a toadstool, who was playing a small flute. When the flute stopped playing all fairies appeared to sing together. Two fairies held hands and spun each other around until their wings lifted them off the ground. Suddenly, right in front of Lucy's eyes, almost touching her face, was Horace dangling from the bracken, he waved and smiled at Lucy and appeared to be tapping the tune coming from the flute with his front right leg.

Lucy decided to leave but not until she had taken in the whole of this magical scene. She also took a picture with her mobile and although her hands shook, she hoped she had it pointed in the right direction. She felt she had to leave and not disturb these incredible and beautiful fairies. Lucy fell into a trance as she walked home and entered her home.

Lucy's mother, who had been making scones in the kitchen for some elderly church members, seemed to know something was not right with her daughter, and called out to her, as Lucy fled up the stairs to her bedroom. Horace had also left the fairy party with Lucy, so as Lucy took her jacket off and went to the bathroom to run a soothing bath.

Horace crawled out of Lucy's jacket pocket. He was tired from the party and decided Lucy could do with his company before she sold him. Perhaps he thought maybe his charming ways would change her mind, and she would keep him, and grow old with him, after all, they could go to the fairy parties together. Horace smiled and crawled onto his pink fluffy cushion.

The two Daisy flower fairies could not find Horace anywhere so decided they would tell him in the morning that Lucy was selling them and not him.

Chapter 2
Sometimes Every Fairy Cries

Fairy Tinkerbell tried hard to ignore the crying coming from the next toadstool to hers. She turned onto her side and wrapped her wings over her ears. It was not at all comfortable, and what was worse, she could still hear the flower fairies crying. It seemed to be getting louder and louder. "Please stop crying, as my ears ache and my bent wings are hurting and will get badly damaged."

"I cannot believe you two happy, Miss Daisy Weed flower fairies, are crying. Do not you recall what true sorrow is?"

The flower fairies remained uncontrolled and sobbed so hard a stream of their tears began to flow at the base of the toadstool. "Now look what you are doing, we are all going to be drowned!"

Snowbell had been called for by Tinkerbell and she flew quickly to the two flower fairies, who had their petal arms around each other trying to comfort each other. "What is wrong, my good flower fairies? Are you ill, in pain? Come, tell me."

Fairy Snowbell's soft caring voice was all that was needed, and they welcomed the open arms of Snowbell.

"We are to be sold. Our photograph has already been taken by Lucy, who needs money for the donkey sanctuary to help Sally."

"Think of all you have learned since you were a bud and ask yourself, would Lucy do such a thing?"

"Well, she has a photograph and sketch of us, and Horace explained that Lucy takes a photograph of things to be sold."

"Lucy is a wonderful girl and if she knows of you, I can assure you she would never sell you. Look how kind she is to Horace and his family."

"She has researched his origin and also cries over how cruel she was as a child to poor Horace, as she was afraid of spiders."

"Yes, fairy Snowbell, you are right, but why sketch us and more so the photograph, how did she see us?"

"Perhaps, flower fairies, it was a moonlit night and as you know fairies stand out in the moonlight."

"Did you notice anyone else in the photograph?"

"Yes, it was the full moon fairy party night, and there appeared lots of fairies, and at least two elders in the background of the photograph."

"So are we all to be sold?" Snowbell looked at the two terrified Miss Daisy Weed flower fairies and began to giggle. "I am only teasing you, what undoubtedly has happened, Lucy has by accident come across our fairy party night and was so surprised to find fairies at the bottom of Mr. Hill's garden, that she took a photograph to prove to herself that she was not dreaming."

"If she told anyone, would they believe her? However, she does have a photograph to prove her words, so we will keep an eye on Lucy to see what she will do with her knowledge."

Snowbell appeared to be deep in thought before she spoke again. "Lucy has seen so many unexplained things, she must have many unanswered questions, and that is how it will stay hopefully! I will check on Lucy many times over the next season, however, flower fairies, I do not wish you to say one word of this to any fairy."

"You can console, Horace; tell him he is a very handsome house spider with elegant legs, and Lucy just wanted a rather nice photograph of him." Snowbell giggled. "He will be so happy to hear that don't you think flower fairies?"

The Daisy flower fairies began to giggle and answered truthfully, "He will love hearing that, fairy Snowbell. We will go and find him."

The flower fairies thanked Snowbell and apologized for their wrong thoughts.

When eventually the flower fairies found Horace hiding behind a large rock, he was sobbing. "Do not cry, Horace, we have looked carefully into your fear of Lucy taking a photograph to sell you." At the sound of the word 'sell', Horace screeched. "Lucy has taken a photograph of you, Horace, as you are such a handsome house spider, with such elegant legs, she would never sell you, Horace."

"I did wonder that, clever little flower fairies. That can be nice and kind to poor Horace sometimes."

Horace waved his two front legs at them and crawled slowly away, but then stopped, and ran back to them. He was still sobbing, but a smile was appearing on his face. "Thank you," was all he could say. He then ran off feeling embarrassed at his weakness for doubting Lucy and overwhelmed at such kindness shown to him by the Daisy flower fairies.

Lucy just wanted to curl up in bed with a hot drink, preferably hot chocolate, and switch her mind off from all these strange happenings. No one would believe her that she had seen fairies and even showing the photograph of the fairies she had taken would still be doubted.

People could do lots of tricks with technology so as to prove it was a genuine photograph would certainly take a long time, and then, of course, there were all the questions she would be asked. She possibly would have to go on television and speak of the sightings of fairies. Then there would be all the visitors wanting to view Mr. Hill's garden with the hope of spotting a fairy or two.

Lucy decided it was a definite no. She would make a note of it in her pink notebook, but that was as far as it would go. *Perhaps it was her imagination playing tricks on her,* she thought, *but quickly threw that thought into the bin.* She knew what she had seen, and the facts were she had seen fairies, and flower fairies, also a green elf, oh and a smiling spider tapping his leg to a tune that was being played on a flute, by a fairy at what appeared to be a fairy party.

Although it was still early evening, Lucy found it impossible to keep awake, even after a warm shower, and a spray of flowery perfume, normally kept for special occasions. She found a pair of cream silk pajamas that were still in their presentation box, given to her for Christmas by her mother, and decided to wear them to lift her mood, to one of positive.

Lucy picked up her pink notebook to make a few notes and tried in vain to fight the urge to sleep.

Chapter 3
Dreams or Reality

Lucy sat up in bed and stared down at the purple duvet. She blinked and rubbed her eyes. Lucy decided to try to go back to sleep and avoid what she was looking at. although the sight before her eyes was beautiful, it was too much to take in.

There were at least a dozen fairies flying over her bed, swooping and landing for a second or two, then off again. Their wings were many shades of pink and lilac. They wore such pretty soft floating dresses, and some wore matching bonnets with flowers tied on with ribbons. They were all smiling.

Lucy began to shake with fear not of the fairies, but of her own eyes. Was she dreaming? She wriggled down under her duvet and closed her eyes. She let her tired head rest on the cotton purple pillowcase for a while, then quickly opened her eyes again. The fairies, some standing and some sitting, were staring straight back at her.

One little fairy flew to Lucy's head and began to stroke her hair. Lucy sat upright and ask, "What have I to do now that I have seen you pretty little fairies?"

Lucy no sooner had asked the question than they all disappeared. She closed her eyes and eventually after much thought fell into a deep sleep.

Although Lucy's dream was quite mixed up, of cruise ships, donkey sanctuaries, and house spiders, what was clear throughout the dream was, the fairies wanted to help her.

Dreams are what make reality work, she thought as she walked up the field toward the donkeys that were coming to greet her. It was a little cold, but a simply wonderful fresh morning, and Lucy's heart was singing with happiness. What a privilege to be able to work and help these donkeys, but where were they? In fact, where was anyone or anything she could recognize?

She screamed for Sally but her voice seemed so strange, and just echoed back at her. She turned around and decided to return to her home, possibly her mother could explain what had happened to all the donkeys and Daisy, the cow. She stared ahead at what appeared to be a very large house and decided to make her way to the front door where she could see a lady polishing a brass knob on the red front door.

Excuse me, I am not sure where I am could you help me. The lady, who was dressed in a maid's outfit, similar to what was worn in Victorian times, beckoned for Lucy to come closer. Lucy stared at the young girl, who could not have been older than herself and explained, "I think I must have been sleepwalking, as I do not recognize where I am."

"I work at the donkey sanctuary and live close to it," she explained.

The maid did not answer but simply took Lucy's hand and lead her into a kitchen at the back of the house, where a roaring fire with some large joint of meat on a rotisserie hung above. She then took a large brass kettle from the side of the fire that sat on a ledge and asked if Lucy would like some tea.

"Come!" the young girl said to Lucy. "Sit in the wooden rocking chair next to the fire and drink some tea, and we will sort this confusion out."

Lucy welcomed the offer and thanked the pretty girl, who was continuing on with her chores. The stove was one of the large old black stoves with a built-in oven, Lucy had seen similar in old farmhouses that had been renovated but kept the Victorian working stove as a character feature.

The maid washed her hands, poured some tea out in a blue and white rather large mug, and handed it to Lucy. She then walked over to a very long pine table that was laden with flour, eggs, milk, and quite a few cooking utensils. Lucy concentrated on the flames in the fire, and although the heat was making her sleepy, turned around to face the busy young girl.

"Where am I?"

"You are in Rogersons' house, the owner of one of the biggest shipping companies. I believe you may be in the wrong house as no donkeys here, but I do know where some are."

"Oh, please take me to them, I am Lucy and my mother will be worried."

"I am called Violet and it is not a donkey, what did you call it a sanctuary, it's where the ponies that go down the mines are kept, I think you mean ponies."

Lucy felt so confused and decided it was all a bad dream and she would wake up.

"They are donkeys, not ponies and yes, it's a sanctuary for donkeys that have been hard-worked and injured."

"I am sixteen and a half years old and I have never heard of such a thing but sounds awfully nice, I often feel so sorry for our four-legged friends, especially the ones that go to war." The young girl wiped a tear from her face and continued, "How can they send these wonderful loyal horses to be killed in such a way and for what?"

Lucy did not answer and her sad thoughts were broken by a young man who entered the kitchen. He rushed to the table where Violet was very busy making something in a pale cream large China bowl. He kissed Violet on the cheek and then looked directly at Lucy and asked, "Why are you dressed like that?"

Lucy, looking down at her cream silk pajamas, began to cry. Violet explained she was sleepwalking and needed to find some donkeys. "Oh" was all the young man could say in reply, and asked Violet where she had put the tin of brass polish.

Violet pointed to a small brass fender cupboard, that was at the right-hand side of the hearth. He lifted the lid, but did not appear to find what he needed. Violet then pointed to the matching cupboard on the left side of the hearth. "You know, it's always kept in one of them, Jack, are you needing boot polish too?"

"No, my darling, just brass polish to shine my buttons. The boots can wait."

A bell rang loudly and Jack in butler's uniform rushed off.

"I am having his baby but no one knows yet as I will lose my job, and my parents will not help me as they can barely feed themselves, but Jack says he will stand by me."

Violet pulled her apron off to show Lucy her rather large tummy. Violet giggled and pulled her dark hair back from her face, which had just dropped out of her maid's headwear, she giggled more and winked her dark eyes flashing with satisfaction and mischief. Lucy could not help a giggle escaping and smiled at Violet.

"Jack is seventeen years older than me. He is the head butler. I have known him for seven months. We will be married shortly. He just has not been able to tell his wife yet."

"Oh goodness, Violet, if I can help you in any way, I will, you and your baby."

"Brat more like it."

Lucy spun around to see an older lady who was dressed similar style to Violet. "He won't marry you, silly girl, they never do, besides its more than possible he will be called up to fight." Violet cried, and the lady patted her arm in sympathy. "Violet girl, wake up and smell the roses, he is a married man with nine children, there is no place in his life for you!"

Violet crying into her white apron ran out through the back door, leading to the garden. Lucy followed and stood in between the rows of washing hanging on the lines. Lucy recognized where she was, it was the back of her mother's house. She looked to the left of the garden and was able to see Sir Arthur and Mr. Hill's garden. It was this large house that confused Lucy, also the era.

Suddenly, Violet stopped crying and indicated for Lucy to listen. Next Violet grasped Lucy's hand and began to run toward the back door. It was then that Lucy could hear what Violet had been listening to. Violet, still holding Lucy's hand, pulled her frantically under the large pine table where she had previously been baking.

The noise above their heads was almost unbearable and all three placed their hands over their ears. Flames roared around them, and the three gasping for air rushed to the door and out into the garden, just in time to see the whole of the roof and the back of the house where they had just run from collapse into rubble. All three were screaming but the noise of the fighter jet above them was all that could be heard.

Violet suddenly shouted, Jack, Jack, and ran to climb over the burning rubble to find him in the house. Lucy ran quickly and wrapped her arms around the sobbing hysterical Violet. "All we can do Violet is pray and wait, come let us hide in that shed."

It was the very same shed, Lucy's bike had been kept in, also the place that Lucy always knew was Horace's, the spider's home. The older lady introduced herself in a trembling quiet voice, almost as if she was scared the pilot above their heads would hear them. "I am Molly Clark, and Violet forgive me for what I said, I am a bitter old maid."

That was the last words Molly Clark spoke and the last words Violet Shepherd would ever hear. The fighter jet had dropped several more bombs, at least two hitting the house once more and a one which landed in the garden. The latter had blasted the door of the shed off and hit Molly and Violet who were the closest to the door.

Lucy lifted the bleeding bodies off her own body and fled out into the garden. All the lines of washing had gone leaving a scattering of burning garments around the garden. Lucy gasped as she watched two men come out of the house with flames coming from them.

Lucy rushed to where a garment from the washing line lay on the grass and ran toward the screaming men. She used the garment to damp out the flames on the men, they appeared to be blinded by the fire, as they frantically ran into the rubble. They collapsed face down on the grass, Lucy knelt beside them, she could see one of the men was Jack.

Although the screaming had stopped, Lucy felt quite confident that they were still alive. It was mainly their backs that appeared badly burned. Lucy instinctively rushed to the washing shed and filled a bucket with cold water. Not knowing what the result would be, she stood a little away from the two men and threw the bucket of cold water over their bare and burnt backs. She was sure it seemed to help them, so she repeated the process.

"Mother, mother, where are you, please help me I am lost."

"I am right here, my darling child, I would never leave you."

Lucy blinked and opened her eyes to see her mother's smiling face. "Mother, I don't want to go back."

"Close your eyes, darling, just rest." Lucy gasped for air, the dust and fumes from the fire were getting worse, and she tried to speak. "Mother, I cannot breathe, the fumes, the fire."

"There is no fire, Lucy, my dear, you are in hospital on a ventilator, you are getting better, darling."

Lucy closed her eyes, not wanting the fear of gasping for air. Although the fire appeared to be out, she still choked on the dust and fumes. Firemen ran across the garden with a hose pipe while others made a man chain passing buckets of water to pour on the smoldering remains of the house. Lucy, feeling so weak and afraid, dropped to her knees on the grass.

"Lucy, we are here in the grass, we have come to help you get better." Two little Daisy flower fairies stared into Lucy's eyes. "We need you to return well to your mother and the correct century, Lucy, you are locked in between times."

"I cannot leave these two men, they are burned so badly, and I must tell someone about Molly and Violet who are dead in my bike shed."

Lucy tried to cry, but she could not, her throat felt so dry and her tongue seemed to be swollen, blocking her airway. If only someone could give me a drink of water. *I will find someone to help the men,* Lucy thought, *or was she speaking to the flower fairies, she really was not at all sure.*

"Lucy, the men are being driven by ambulance to the local Infirmary. They will be well again." The flower fairies paused to give time for Lucy to digest what they were saying.

"Oh, I thought I saw them on the grass when I returned, I must be dreaming, then Violet and Molly, can you help me to tell someone, please, and Horace, was poor Horace in the shed, I know he lives there." Lucy's voice trailed off and her eyes closed, searching for sleep.

Lucy gasped and opened her eyes. A dark-haired man was placing something into her dry mouth, she gasped and tried to push his hand and the instrument away from her mouth, Lucy's mother spoke gently to her dying child. "Let the doctor help you, darling; do not fight it, my darling; do not leave me, my angel."

"Lucy, come back to us." The flower fairies sweet gentle voice made Lucy want to smile. "You are dreaming and also hallucinating. You only thought Violet and Molly were dead, go and see for yourself." They paused to give Lucy a little time to reply.

"Do I go back to the shed? Are they still there?"

"Lucy, it's all a dream and unless you give it all a happy ending, it will become a nightmare. You can climb the rubble and enter into the kitchen and see for yourself, and remember happy endings."

Lucy obediently climbed the rubble, Molly was rubbing dust off the kitchen table and Violet had her hand in a red biscuit tin, the ladies chatted happily. Lucy ran first to Molly, hugging her and then to Violet. "I thought the blast had killed you both, I have been so very sad."

Violet giggled. "It will take more than a little fighter jet to finish us off, ain't that right, Molly?"

"Aye, lass, here have a cup of tea, I made it for Jack and his handyman but Doctor wanted them checked out at the Infirmary." Molly handed a cup of tea and then said with a big smile on her face. "We have something very happy to tell you, Lucy. Are you sitting down?"

"Yes, and I cannot wait to hear what it is."

Molly, still smiling, replied, "Doctor also examined Violet to make sure the bairn had not been harmed. It appears Violet is farther on than she thought, as the doctor asked what Violet had planned to enable her to keep her baby, Violet cried as she then saw the reality of having a baby. Violet is moving in with my sister and I, bairn will be fine, a little spoiled but fine, my sister is in a wheelchair, trouble with her legs, so Violet can help my sister Doris."

Violet seemed delighted with the solution. "Baby and I will have our own room, and I can cook and clean and go to church on a Sunday."

Molly wiped a tear from her eyes and sipped her tea. "To have a baby in the house, I cannot begin to tell you what that will mean to my sister and I." She wiped another tear. "The house was left to my sister and I by our aunty Beth. It is such a large house, more like a mansion. We also were left a nice tidy packet, and that little baby will go without naught."

Lucy kissed them both and gently patted Violet's belly.

"Lucy, Lucy, time to return, all is sorted here, such happy endings, if you look hard enough you will always find a happy ending. Come, Lucy, your mother is waiting and praying for your return."

Lucy's eyes flickered and a doctor thanked the almighty and said, "We have her back. Lucy will live."

"A team of doctors and nurses who had attended Lucy night and day for the past two months applauded."

"She needs plenty of rest but your daughter will recover. Perhaps you should go home and sleep and return later."

Lucy did make a full recovery, and within two weeks was managing to do some light work at the donkey sanctuary. She remembered all, especially the Daisy flower fairies, she decided to keep that to herself, although it was certainly made a note of in her pink book.

Chapter 4
Happy Endings

Lucy was still feeling weak even thou it had been over a month since she had left the hospital. She walked slowly up the field toward the waiting and watching donkeys ready for their breakfast. The field felt quite a struggle to Lucy, far more than normal, so she decided to sit and rest, as she turned to look for a place to relax for a while, the earth started to move closer to her face, and Lucy hit the ground with quite a thump.

Snowdrops trotted down toward Lucy who appeared to be asleep, but as he spotted Sally and Johnny running up the field toward Lucy, he decided something more important than a tasty carrot was happening, Snowdrops could still view Lucy from where he stood close to Mr. Hill's garden wall.

"What is it, Snowdrop?" Snowbell asked as she spotted a sad Snowdrops, who normally would have been near the top of the field at this time in the morning, awaiting breakfast. Fairy Snowbell decided to travel with Lucy in the ambulance as Sally and Johnny appeared to stay to attend to the hungry donkeys.

"What is it Lucy? Are you ill again, sad?"

"Yes, I am so sad. Can you help me?"

"Yes, I believe I can, Lucy."

"You see, I know all you fairies are real and live at the bottom of Mr. Hill's Garden, and I also happen to know Horace personally."

"Why are you not surprised? Am I meant to know? If so, why?"

"Yes, Lucy, we the fairies and Elfvil, the elf, all knew you could see us and hear us."

"I believe it all started with our naughty, yet lovable spider, Horace."

"Is that correct?"

"Yes, it is correct." Lucy burst into tears as she answered, and the ambulance crew rushed to her comfort and called the driver to go slower to the hospital. Snowbell was hidden by a thick red blanket which was laid over shivering Lucy.

"Lucy, was it after you threw Horace on the fire that you started to love him?"

"Yes," Lucy sobbed and speaking with her mind to this adorable little fairy that kept sneezing and plaiting her hair. "How could I have done such a cruel thing, his poor legs."

"Look, dear Lucy, at how much good has come from that sad experience."

"You have not just grown up, but developed knowledge, even passed exams in Entomology."

"We need you, Lucy, the world needs you, never be sad when there is so much love in your heart for the insects, creatures, and animals."

Lucy spoke her thoughts, which she had kept bottled up deep inside her, "I sometimes wish I was in a university with my friends, having a great time, why do I not, I am missing such a lot, and yet I love the donkey sanctuary, and Sally and Johnny and everyone here, but why am I not enjoying myself like others of my age?"

Snowbell giggled. "You sound so like a little Daisy Weed, I know that became two, but unfortunately we cannot clone you."

"There is only one Lucy, one very special Lucy, who will use her imagination and knowledge to help the world. You will not miss anything; you will be fulfilled with your life."

"Which has a very happy ending."

Lucy arrived at the hospital with a huge smile on her face. Doctors examined Lucy and found her to be exhausted.

"Lucy!"

Lucy opened her eyes and saw the youngest and most handsome doctor. She smiled up at Samuel Sheridan. Lucy's eyes had never looked so bright, and the doctor smiled back as he noticed not only how beautiful this young girl was, but her incredible eyes. "You don't mind me calling you Lucy, do you?"

"No, not at all. I am sorry I am troubling you. I believe I may have fallen asleep. Was I asleep?"

"I believe you were found unconscious by your friends, so let's have a good look at you, oh also I have been told you are recovering from this dreadful virus."

"Yes, that is correct, will I be alright, Doctor. For some reason, I suddenly feel a little better, will I be able to ring my mother and ask her to collect me, you see Doctor, I have not finished feeding the donkeys."

At that, Lucy fell fast asleep. Doctor Sheridan stared in amazement as Lucy appeared to be wide awake one minute, and unbelievably sound asleep the next. He walked off toward the cafeteria and decided to sit and collect his thoughts. All Doctor Sheridan could think of was Lucy's beautiful face smiling up at him.

,He sent a text to Cynthia a junior nurse, canceling their date on Saturday, and decided he would start and follow his dreams instead of trying to please his friends by following the trend, to date most of the nursing staff. Well, they can think what they want, I am not going, and I won't be dating any girl unless they make my heart flutter like that adorable Lucy had just done.

Samuel would have eaten a sandwich or salad but today it was coffee only, and a fast heartbeat as he thought of Lucy. He needed to go back to the ward Lucy had been admitted to and make a decision on what was to be done with Lucy, the sleeping beauty.

He smiled and walked briskly back to ward 2 and spotted Lucy's fair hair hanging out from the top of the white bed linen. She was still sound asleep and Doctor Samuel, tempted to leave her sleeping, stopped the personal side creeping in. He called a nurse to pull a screen around Lucy's bed and asked a senior doctor to help him with the new patient.

"She is exhausted and needs rest." Doctor Samuel Sheridan said to his senior, who totally agreed.

"Yes, two days in bed should do it, I believe. She has obviously gone back to work too soon. Do you know what she does?"

"Zoo, I think, as she mentioned feeding donkeys, oh it's possibly a sanctuary, not a zoo."

"Well, we can ask her now!"

"Hullo, Lucy, welcome to the British Flag Hospital. How are you, Lucy?"

"I feel so very well, thank you, and need to get back to the donkey sanctuary. I have not fed them and they will be so hungry."

At that, Lucy fell fast asleep, and two fascinated doctors decided another coffee and a chat was in order.

Samuel followed everything he had been taught at university. one very important aspect was never to involve personal doctors and patients, no matter how difficult. Samuel had barely touched his coffee and it was starting to cool. Doctor Lenardo broke the silence and also Doctor Samuel's thought pattern. "You have hardly touched your coffee Samuel, and if you do not mind me saying, this silence has been a total waste of my time!"

Doctor Lenardo who placed very important pauses between his words for effect, as taught him by Professors he admired, got the desired effect from Samuel he was looking for. "Oh, sorry, you are right, I am a little lost off at present, and extremely rude. I ask your pardon."

"Granted, now, young man, spill. Let me help you, Samuel."

"It's patient confidentiality. I am in love with my patient, or if I am not, then I am under one almighty spell, and require immediate help, as I fear I am going to jeopardize all my years of hard work, lock me away and throw the key away dear Lenardo."

Lenardo looked over his gold-rimmed spectacles and frowned. "Good heavens, Samuel. You are so dramatic, it's not help from me you require, it's an audition for one of Sir William Shakespeare's plays, you appear to be wasting your talent here!"

Samuel felt no need to reply, drank the remainder of the now cold coffee, patted his senior and close friend endearingly on his back, and left, after placing ten pounds to cover the coffee.

However, Lenardo had struck a chord in him and brought his feet firmly down on the hospital-tiled floor. He headed to the gentleman's room where he splashed cold water onto his face and did feel much better. He walked fast down the corridor toward the ward Lucy was in. Lucy was sitting up and smiling. He walked over to her.

"Lucy, we require some information from you, your doctor's name and where he or she can be contacted, and also your age and address, etc. I will send a nurse over to take various blood samples and some brief information from you, we should be able to get what we require from your medical center."

Lucy smiled and asked, "Please, Doctor, may I return today? I really do feel very well?"

"If your tests come back normal and there is no underlying reason for this episode, then we will consider that. However, you had previously been very ill with the virus for quite a long time, all this must be taken into consideration, but I can promise you, that you will not be kept here longer than necessary as we need the bed."

Doctor Samuel walked away happy with himself, he had handled that very professionally. *Doctor Lenardo who was entering the ward as Samuel left, welcomed the wink and smile from his friend, and decided to invite him over on Friday night for a game of tennis and a few cold beers, or cold coffees,* he thought, and smiled to himself.

Chapter 5
Who Said Romance Was Dead

Doctor Lenardo smiled across the dinner table at his friend and junior colleague, Samuel. He had met Samuel for the first time over a year ago, and had taken to him immediately, his professional and enthusiastic outlook reminded him of himself, when he had first qualified as a medical doctor.

Doctor Samuel Sheridan was respected and loved by all the medical staff, with a fan club of nurses hoping for a date. Samuel always kept his distance, although once or twice had been caught off guard, and felt rather mean making a quick exit from some nurses' or doctors' party.

Joseph Lenardo walked around the dining table, and taking the bottle of malbec from the three-tiered Victorian dumb waiter, poured Samuel a large glass. "Now, my friend, spill. I want to hear exactly where you are in your head, over our strawberry blonde patient."

Samuel had hardly slept in three nights, his thoughts returning and returning to Lucy. "I will be alright, I fear I am losing my marbles as I do not even know her surname,

I have to start and focus more on my profession, then I can make her disappear from my rather tired mind."

Samuel paused, and forgetting all the warnings on the walls around the hospital, drank every drop of the wine, and held out his glass for a refill. "Steady on, old chum. She is not worth a liver transplant."

The two friends laughed, and Samuel's glass was once again filled to the brim. "I am afraid that I may step out of line, Joseph, I am already doing what I class as unhealthy, scrutinizing on the internet, well not too drastic I guess, more like looking at donkeys."

They both laughed without stopping for quite some time, and Joseph decided to get Samuel into a more serious conversation, asking him what he thought of Higgins. "Doctor Higgins, although a little insensitive, I rather like, and the patients certainly trust him, he has a lovely bedside manner and is able to explain in depth to patients their operation, yes he is definitely an improvement on Doctor Graham."

"More salmon, or salad, you don't want to fade away, which I fear may be a possibility."

"Thank you, I would love more, my favorite as you know, and you are right of course, I have not been eating just pining away, and for what, a pretty face and a girl who has a soft voice, and gorgeous skin, and eyes that light up the sky."

"OK, Samuel, that's enough, eat up and drink your wine, for I fear I have lost you and also my will to live."

The laughter appeared to continue on into the early hours of the morning. Joseph had already made up the bed in the spare room, which was called Samuel's room. He went to the corner cabinet in the lounge and took a bottle of scotch he had purchased earlier in the evening.

"Come, Samuel, let's have a whiskey on the balcony. I have something of great interest to tell you. In fact, best take the bottle with us, as I fear you may need another one. Our little donkey lady works at Brown's Donkey Sanctuary, previously Hill's Donkey Sanctuary. It is her best friend Sally, recently married, who owns the sanctuary."

Joseph took a sip of the whiskey and continued, "She is quite a remarkable young lady, and ran the sanctuary almost single-handed when her friends married. They went on honeymoon on board the cruise ship Johnny Brown, Sally's husband, worked on as a pastry chef, they returned home a lot later than planned due to the ship being docked because of the virus, that has swept the world."

"Lucy has a love of spiders and insects and has studied and qualified as an entomologist."

The two men had sat in silence for some time, Samuel digesting what he was hearing and Joseph needing to switch off for a while. "Come, let's talk more another time, but now let's listen to Mozart."

"Just one question please, then no more I promise. How do you know all this Joseph?"

"It's our mutual friend who knows the family personally. Doctor Gerard Bernstein is our informant, seemingly his wife Lisa played the organ at their wedding. Small world would you agree?"

The conversation moved to important patient affairs, some they could turn into light humorous conversations, and others far more troubling seemed to devour their precious moments and lead to silence. There had been so many sad cases in their hospital lately, mainly caused by the current situation, as the virus was still very much a daily occurrence.

They could only pray and use every ounce of knowledge they had, but somehow the virus was in control more and more, as different variants of the virus were detected around the world. Vaccines had commenced months ago and the news appeared to be fixed for a while on the numbers of vaccinated people.

It was hopeful, and all who worked at their hospital went around with a very optimistic approach, and yet their wards appeared to be filling up once again with different strains of the virus. The two men ended the evening with a cup of tea and a chocolate wafer biscuit.

Samuel woke early and decided to take a coffee to his friend, who he had heard in the kitchen hours after he had gone to bed. Joseph was sitting up in bed, reading a medical manuscript on past viruses. Samuel placed the coffee down carefully beside a notebook and pen.

"Thank you, Samuel. You're a good chap when you're not drooling over some pretty patient." The two men laughed and decided to delay a game of tennis by an hour or two. "Perhaps we could have a morning walk around the market, buy some fruit I don't appear to have much."

So the morning agreed upon, Samuel went back to his bed, drank his coffee, and although wide awake, enjoyed resting his body.

Walking around the market turned out to be a perfect decision as they spotted quite a few doctors they knew doing the same. They were all so happy to see each other and touch base with the current affairs. They sat outside a very trendy little pup that had canopies of bright yellow shielding them from the sun and watched the swans on the river, it was such a lovely day. The men laughed loudly as each one made humorous comments.

"Wow, Samuel, did you see that stunning girl on ward 5? She had just been admitted."

Samuel's heart started to beat with a thunder he had never known, and yet replied a little too dismissive to convince any of the men listening, that he meant what he was saying. "Oh no, I cannot say I did, Jake, I had a very busy week."

The men merely raised their eyebrows in disbelief. "You, my friend, appear to require an eye test!"

Joseph quickly moved the conversation on, with an offer of more tea or coffee and fresh grapes. The men all decided to lunch at a very popular Italian restaurant not far from where they were. A very organized Toby in the group of men held up his mobile to the men and telephone the restaurant in advance.

It was all so splendid, the restaurant lived up to its five stars, and the wine flowed, however not for two of the younger doctor's that were on call at the hospital. The men, now down to six, decided to round the afternoon off with a boat trip on the river. More wine and a plate full of French toast was exactly the remedy for these mentally exhausted young clever doctors.

Samuel, feeling rested and refreshed after the weekend, walked into the hospital with a spring in his step. He could not quite work out if he was happy because he had so enjoyed the weekend, or that he may manage miraculously a conversation with Doctor Bernstein.

The latter thought he tried to dismiss, as it seemed a crazy thought. Very rarely would he ever see Doctor Bernstein as he was highly qualified and appeared to work the opposite side of the hospital to himself, on the children's ward. Also, he was a very private man who never ever joined any of the doctors for a drink. He always politely refused and never gave an excuse or explanation. Just a no, but thank you, guys.

So, Samuel decided to shelve that thought. He would somehow live in the hope that his friend Lenardo would find a way. As he entered ward 5, he noticed Lucy's bed was empty, perhaps she had been moved, as he was sure she would not have been well enough to leave just yet.

He was walking down the ward, full mask and visor, plus plastic covering over his hospital uniform, as he noticed an urgent admittance. The stretcher was ushered at speed to the wards, adapted for severe cases of the deadly virus. The nurses wheeling the patient were complete with ropes and masks that resembled something in a horror movie. Samuel decided to look closer and see if he was required to help.

"Samuel," the voice calling his name almost shook his very soul. Samuel looked across the corridor to where Doctor Bernstein stood, he appeared to be frantic. "Go with the stretcher, Samuel, please, it's Lisa, my wife, she is dying, help her please, Samuel. I will get Lenardo."

As Samuel rushed to obey the orders, he heard in the distance, I found her lying in the greenhouse. Samuel did not stop to acknowledge Doctor Bernstein's explanation of where he had found his wife, but had all he needed organized and on board to help with poor Lisa Bernstein's admittance. He stayed at Lisa's bedside for over an hour, checking regularly on her progress, which was not at all good.

Doctor Bernstein arrived with Lenardo, and the two stood at the foot of Lisa's bed reading the notes, some Samuel had just written. "She never goes out unless to play the organ for some church service, or," but Doctor Bernstein broke down and wept. "She is my life, my salvation. Please do not let her die. I love her and I cannot live without her," he sobbed uncontrollably. "Oh, the animals," he gasped.

Samuel led Doctor Bernstein out of the ward and took him to a quiet room normally used when doctors have to inform relatives of bad news. Samuel was given a sweet tea in a plastic cup by one of the nurses who had heard the sadness in Doctor Bernstein's voice. "I have left my front door open as I came with the ambulance. We have dogs and cats, they will get out onto the road. They will not understand, they adore her so, please help me, what am I to do."

Samuel needed no time to reply. "You stay at Lisa's bedside, play her soft music, she will respond to what she knows and plays, and I will drive immediately to your house and make sure all animals are safely inside, then feed them. Do you have a cleaner, or good neighbor? I will take them with me and organize something. I promise you, I will sort it all."

Samuel left to follow the instructions given by Doctor Bernstein, he would drive to the cleaner's cottage and then together with her sort these animals out. Hannah just lives along the lane from the Bernstein's residence in an old lodge cottage. She had seen the ambulance and wondered what had happened and wondered even more when she spotted one of the Bernstein's dogs out and Scarlet and Ginger the cats sitting outside the main gate.

The two cats she had managed to get them into the cozy kitchen that had a log-burning stove but the black toy poodle ran along the lane. Hannah had caught up with the nervous little dog and took her back into her lodge. She had fed the cats in the kitchen and the little dog in her own kitchen, although it did not eat more than a mouthful.

"Samuel," Hannah said, in a very upset voice, "these little animals adore Lisa, they are fretting, come let's get this little dog back to its home and check on the other dogs, also Ginger and Scarlet will need more food, Oh and swans."

Samuel's breath was taken away when he saw Doctor Gerard Bernstein's stately house. He had heard that Bernstein's residence was something special, but this was far more than he ever imagined. As they entered the kitchen two dogs rushed in expectation of their master's return and dropped their tails when they discovered Hannah and this stranger.

"Come girls," Samuel called out to the sad dogs that were retreating back to their basket that held a very cozy tartan Mackintosh rug. Samuel walked over to the basket at the side of the log fire and patted the friendly dogs, Ginger fearing the worse for Lisa, but seeing a kind young man, walked over to Samuel followed by a very shy Scarlet, and rubbed up against Samuel.

Samuel was on his knees patting the dogs and stroking the cats when Hannah called out to them to come and have their lunch. *At first, there was very little interest as the ambulance had taken their appetite totally away, but Ginger spotted sardines in his dish, mm,* he thought, *she must not know its Monday, I never get sardines on a Monday as had them for Sunday lunch.*

So, once Ginger started to eat, Scarlett soon followed and then the dogs nibbled a bit of their tuna, pasta, and cheese. Samuel looked at these delicious dinners given to the animals on China plates and bowls. Hannah spotting Samuel looking, explained, they are all vegetarians, and very spoilt. They both laughed and Hannah Stacey handed Samuel a cup of tea, which was most welcomed by Samuel.

"I guess, Hannah, the animals are their children." Samuel looked directly at Hannah's expressive brown eyes. Hannah looked like a very wise woman, who in her 60s had seen a lot of life. "What is it, Hannah? Is there something I should know, are you wanting to tell me something but feel you should not?"

"Yes, that is exactly it." Hannah walked over to the stove, picked up the large brown teapot that sat on the top of the stove, and poured herself another cup of tea before offering a cup of tea to Samuel. Samuel decided he had to pursue what Hannah knew.

"Tell me please, Hannah, right now while we drink a cup of tea in Lisa's cozy kitchen, she is on a ventilator and fighting for her life."

That was enough for Hannah, who burst into tears. "I love that girl like she was my own, and I know she is pregnant. She was waiting a few more weeks before she told Gerard, as she had miscarried a year ago."

Lisa never told Gerard, as he had so much work at his hospital, and she blamed herself for the miscarriage. She had been crawling around on wet grass, in a jungle, looking for a new fern. When she returned home, she was ill and believed she had a fever, I do believe it was Doctor Joseph, someone, who saw her at the hospital and broke the dreadful news, that she had been pregnant, and lost the baby.

She could not have been more than two months when she lost the baby, she is now almost four months. Although it's hard to believe she is pregnant at all, she is painfully thin. Hannah was still very upset so Samuel decided to break her thought pattern and ask a few questions that could throw some insight into Lisa and her pregnancy.

"Tell me, Hannah, does she have any eating disorder?"

"No, not at all. She eats lots. When I remind her to eat, you see she gets carried away with her animals and plants, and just forgets." Hannah smiled and gave a little giggle and added, "Doctor Gerard and Lisa would fade away if it was not for my cooking. I love cooking and they love eating my food. It is so rewarding."

"Come, look in here." Hannah led Samuel from the kitchen and into the larder and opened a floor-to-ceiling American freezer. It was full of various frozen cooked meals, all neatly stacked in blue and white serving bowls. They were also alphabetically labeled by Hannah. "They do entertain so there is enough food in there to serve a regiment."

"If I miss Lisa which is not often as I am serving their breakfast five days out of seven, but if I do, say I have a flu or Lisa has gone out early, then I ring and remind her what to take out the freezer and how long it should be in the oven."

"Hannah, do not upset yourself. Lisa sounds like a very lucky lady to have you close by looking after her. My guess is she will recover from this dreadful virus." Hannah smiled and Samuel made his way to the door, leaving his calling card displaying his mobile number on the pine kitchen table. "Telephone me if there are any problems with the animals, or even if it is something significant, you remember that may help."

Samuel parked his car in the doctor's 's private car park and walked with haste to Ward 5. He was stopped quite a few times and given patient information and informed of new admittance, but no one mentioned Lisa Bernstein. Entering Ward 5 it was very much as he had left it less than two hours ago. Gerard sat at Lisa's bedside. All staff, including Gerard, were completely gowned.

Samuel pulled a chair up beside Gerard and spoke clearly through his mask and visor. "All is well, Gerard, at your home, the animals are all back inside, mainly in the warm kitchen, also they have all been fed. Hannah is staying with them and tidying up, so you have not a thing to worry about apart from Lisa, who I'm sure, Gerard, is a very strong lady, who will pull through."

Gerard did not answer but looked up and stared at Samuel, tears filling his eyes. "Come now, Gerard, have faith look at her chart. Lisa's temperature is coming down already. Has anyone examined Lisa yet?"

"No, No."

"Then would you allow me to do so, Sir." Gerard seemed to automatically stand up and move away from the bed. "Thank you, Sir."

Samuel watched as a very tired Doctor Gerard Bernstein left the ward, and then indicated to a passing nurse to pull the curtain around Lisa and help him with the examination. Samuel pressed gently on Lisa's stomach, then placed a stethoscope and listened for the baby's heartbeat. Samuel's look of surprise was indicated to the nurse, who understood and quickly went off to find a nurse to bring a scan and radiographer.

Ten minutes later, Samuel had confirmed his findings, there were two strong heartbeats. "Can you bring Doctor Bernstein into the cubicle immediately?"

Gerard Bernstein ran across the ward in seconds, thinking the worse. At first, he could not register what was happening, and why were they taking a scan of his wife's abdomen. He looked at Samuel in confusion and required an explanation.

"Listen and look at the screen," Samuel pointed to where one heartbeat came from, and before Gerard almost passed out pointed to where another heartbeat came from. The two men indicated with their arms a hug.

Two hours later, a very strong Lisa was moved to a private ward. The virus was leaving and Lisa was improving, her strength coming back.

Chapter 6
Depth of Love

Oh Lucy, Oh Lucy, my love, Samuel thought as his excitement at telling Gerard Bernstein all the good news, including all the animals safely home, suddenly turned to emptiness as he thought of Lucy.

"Where are you, my love?" he whispered to himself. If ever there was proof of telepathy, it was now. Samuel's mobile and on-call bleeper was left in his locker, so when a nurse waved to him and indicated a telephone call. Samuel was most confused, his first thoughts went to Hannah and then to his parents.

His first thought was correct, as he heard Hannah's voice at the other end of the line. "I am so sorry, Doctor Samuel, to trouble you, but I have a young girl by the name of Lucy in the kitchen, she has said there is a delivery of at least six retired racehorses, and one with a healing broken leg that has to have a vet on hand when the delivery comes, which is in thirty minutes time, 2.30 PM."

"I am sorry I really did not know a thing about this, certainly, Lisa never told me, as she knows I would have told her straight that she was taking far too much on in her present state, er, condition. Lucy is one of the partners of Hill's, er, Brown's Donkey Sanctuary."

"Yes, yes, I know of her. Tell her to ring the vets and sort a vet to be at Bernstein's and give her some tea, or broth. She is not in the best of health. Then tell her to wait, I will be there in time. Hannah, can you make a sandwich or two? I am going to miss lunch and will be working very late tonight at the hospital, also not sure what Gerard has eaten. I doubt very little, the state he was in when I left."

Hannah felt proud of the role she had been given. She felt so trusted, as Lisa always made her feel, although why she had not mentioned the horses' arrival was a bit of a mystery. They would need to check the stables, as Hannah turned around she was just in time to see Lucy pass the window pointing to the stables, she was talking on her mobile to a local veterinarian they used for the donkey sanctuary.

Samuel arrived with a few minutes to spare and a little too early for the broccoli and Stilton soup, which was still being heated on the stove. "Which way to the stables?"

Samuel almost ran in the direction he had been given but noticing the mud on the old cobbles, decided to walk quickly and carefully instead. Lucy had moved quite a bit of old kitchen furniture from the stables when Samuel arrived. Lucy greeted Samuel with a big smile and a question.

"Please we need to brush these stables out and disinfect them before we place the straw. They are lovely stables and have not been neglected at all although they cannot have been used in at least 4 years."

Samuel picked up a huge sweeping brush from the corner of the stables and began to quickly brush up the dust and dirt. I have straw arriving with the vet and also hay. He should be arriving shortly, she glanced at her large wristwatch. "Please can you stay a while, I have just realized who you are, you are my lovely Doctor?"

"Samuel, mam, at your service," he smiled at Lucy and spoke in a doctor's tone. "Lucy, we do have to sort this for Lisa and Doctor Bernstein, then I must return to the hospital and you to your bed. First, the horses, which I believe I can hear arriving at this very moment."

Lucy was out of the stables and running toward Hannah who was talking to a vet and a large man who had stepped out of his large horse wagon. Lucy quickly had the wagon containing eight retired racehorses directed to where the stable block was.

Hannah, relieved all was being taken care of, returned to her stove. Seven horses, after being thoroughly checked by Paul, were placed in the field adjoining the stables. Paul had decided to give three of the horses their yearly vaccine, the papers showed this had not been done. However, Paul was happy with the care and fitness these horses had obviously been given.

Cinderella, the horse with the broken leg, was so grateful for the gentle touch of Paul and rubbed her nose up and down on Paul's green tunic. Samuel was so taken by the scene, he had never had any time with animals in his youth, not even a visit to the zoo. Every penny his father made was placed into savings for his son's future.

So Samuel breathed in the atmosphere. It was a long time later before Cinderella was placed into her stable on the clean fresh-smelling straw. She had eaten and drank so the vet decided to leave and return at midday tomorrow to check.

Lucy smiled at Samuel and the two walked without words toward the open door where Hannah stood. "I have made salmon and cucumber and coleslaw and pease-pudding sandwiches for you and Doctor Gerard." Hannah placed the container beside Samuel. "Will you now please have a bowl of soup before it totally boils away."

Samuel answered for them both, "Yes, Hannah, Lucy, and I would love a bowl of your delicious-smelling soup."

"Are all the horses in the field for the night as I have no idea how to put horses back into their stables, hard enough putting hens in the pens for the night?" Hannah asked.

Lucy looked up from her soup and smiled. "I am placing them inside after my soup. They have come quite a distance and they will just want to be in their new homes and sleep."

Samuel shot Lucy a glance of chastisement and added. "Lucy, I fear my dear it is you that should be in bed, but tell me Lucy dear girl, how did you know about the racehorses arriving, when was Lisa able to tell you?"

Lucy spoke slowly and clearly, her eyes avoiding his, "The Fairies, they told me!"

Chapter 7
Coincidences

Samuel left at the same time as Lucy neither had finished their soup, much to Hannah's disappointment. Samuel praised and thanked Hannah, but explained how worried he suddenly felt. "I have been away from my post too long, Hannah, patients need me, I will see if I am needed here tomorrow by Gerard. I am sure, Hannah, I will be here again enjoying your soup, which is truly wonderful."

"Take care, Hannah, and thank you." Lucy had cycled on her old lilac bike and was about to leave as she also felt worried over her donkeys. "Hannah I will be here in the morning at seven to let the horses out into the field and feed them, will you be here to feed the other animals?"

Hannah felt happy and needed once again.

Samuel headed straight to the private ward Lisa had been moved to for recovery. Gerard sat close to Lisa, who although recovering, looked incredibly ill. Gerard's face was close to Lisa's mouth as she tried to whisper something to him. Gerard looked at Samuel and asked. "Can you make out what my wife is trying to say please?"

Samuel came close and bent over the bed to listen to Lisa, who appeared agitated. "Horses, horses, help! Horses, house!"

Samuel smiled at Gerard and patted Lisa's arm with his protective glove. "Lisa, all is well. The racehorses are in their stable for the night, all fed and watered, so please do not upset yourself. Your household furry animals are also fed and lying in a very cozy kitchen. The vet has checked all the horses, including one with a broken leg, called Cinderella. They are all very handsome, oh, and fully vaccinated."

"Lucy will be at the stables to let them into the field and feed them early tomorrow. In fact, Lucy has done everything, even making sure the stables were spotless and disinfected."

All Lisa could do was given a sigh of relief and drift back into a deep sleep. Gerard walked behind Samuel and out of the ward, leaving Lisa to sleep peacefully. The two doctors both looked quite exhausted, although they were both working late. Samuel would finish after midnight and try to catch up on his work. Gerard was just wanting to stay close to Lisa as it was still early days and a very slow recovery ahead. They ordered some strong coffee, and it was then that Samuel remembered the sandwiches in his car. "I have just remembered, Doctor Gerard, that I have salmon and cucumber sandwiches for you. Hannah has made, also coleslaw and pease-pudding." Samuel smiled as he said the contents of the sandwiches.

"Coleslaw and pease-pudding sandwiches are most pleasant, Lisa introduced me to them, they are special. In fact, that is exactly what I would love to eat, kindly go and fetch them, we can sit here and eat them in comfort, but first tell me who told you about the horses?"

Samuel stood up to leave and fetch the sandwiches from his car, but suddenly turned around and faced Gerard and smiled, "The fairies, Sir."

There was complete silence as they ate the sandwiches and drank the strong coffee. Both feeling refreshed, Samuel started to put the pieces together for Gerard. "They are retired racehorses, eight of them, one with a broken leg to mend, they a truly splendid, and I do believe Lisa has saved their lives."

"Yes, Samuel, that sounds just like what my darling wife would do! I cannot thank you enough for all you have done, and I will not forget either."

"It has been a distraction from the virus and also a pleasure, meeting Hannah and all the animals, I was starting to feel quite at home, Sir." Samuel smiled at Gerard and suddenly, they were close friends, as they had shared so much. Samuel broke the silence by adding. "Plus, I know where most things are kept in your kitchen, oh and stables are second home to me."

The two doctors laughed for the first time in what seemed like an eternity. "I am here, Sir, if you need me for anything further, besides it was lovely seeing Lucy again, she was my patient for a short time, virus weakness, but she seemed very bright and happy today, especially around those magnificent horses."

Samuel needed to speak more of Lucy and so continued dreamily, "She organized the veterinarian and it's good she did as two needed their vaccine. She is incredible, studies spiders."

"Yes, I have heard from Lisa she is a remarkable young lady. Her father, I believe, is Judge Arthur."

"Not the Judge Arthur?"

"Yes, Samuel, that is him."

Dr. Gerard, feeling it was time to depart the rather almost too friendly conversation, stood up and thanked Samuel once again, and then took his leave. Samuel was glad he was working late, as he knew he would never sleep tonight. He wished he had been not so friendly and more respectful with his conversation. Plus, Lucy was also swirling around in his head.

He decided he would put work first and not think of these doubts, but no matter how hard he tried Lucy, Coleslaw sandwiches, the fairies, and the familiarity of animals to say nothing of what was in Doctor Gerard's kitchen cupboard, swirled aimlessly around in his mind. When Samuel's bleeper went off, he felt relieved and made his way to ward five as new arrivals were admitted and wheeled in.

By 11 PM, Samuel sat down to drink a coffee and reflect. Had he missed something? But answering his own question, he felt quite confident all or mainly all was up to date.

His mind returned to Lucy, even in her working denim overalls she looked so lovely he thought and recalled how they had worked together cleaning the stables. He decided another once around the wards, to check the new admittance, and then take a shower before driving home. Samuel placed the coffee back on the table untouched and decided on a milky hot chocolate instead.

It had seemed such a long day to Samuel, and as he stretched out in bed trying to recall his time at Gerard Bernstein's home, it became harder and harder to recall, so he relented and gave into sleep. He was woken at seven by the alarm, and as he made his way to the kitchen, he checked the landline telephone for any messages.

There were three messages on the answering machine, one regarding one of his patients that had been moved to another hospital, a rather hurried message from Doctor Gerard, again thanking him and asking could he please check the stable lock and make sure Lucy manages to sort the horses. The third message was also from Gerard. "Sorry I had to check a patient urgently. I just wanted to ask if you could also make sure the larder is full, as I don't want Lisa to worry about anything. She woke during the night to ask about the stable lock. Thank you, Samuel."

Samuel sat at his breakfast bar drinking coffee, he was neither dressed nor showered for the working day ahead and yet he could not wait for the day to begin.

Samuel was at Bernstein's stables checking the lock when Lucy arrived on her bike. He smiled as she approached the stable door. Her hair was in a hurried ponytail, as part of her hair had not made it into the pink elastic band. She wore pink trainers with gold leather decorative bits covered in mud. Black joggers, and a fluffy pink zipped jacket.

She looked as if she had been to a disco and returned home over the fields. Lucy had never considered her dress sense, even though from being an infant her mother had always bought very pretty clothing for her attractive daughter. Lucy was the opposite of her mother, and would rather walk the fields cold and barefooted as long as the animals were taken care of. The older Lucy became, the more it became clear; this was Lucy and no one would change her, although Lucy's mother had a feeling plenty would try.

The retired racehorses seemed to be drawn to Lucy in a way Samuel felt he could never describe. *Like magic,* he thought. He left Lucy to sort the horses that appeared to be at home with their surroundings and decided to fix the new lock he had purchased on his journey. It was the largest lock Gregory's hardware store had, and without the appropriate tools, took quite some time to screw onto the hardwood of the stables.

Samuel was pleased he had succeeded with the lock, as he was worried about the time, as he needed to get to the hospital. It someone felt a little wrong to be struggling with a lock when people were sick and dying and needing his help. In a state of haste and panic, Samuel rushed to his silver Honda and drove off, giving a toot of the horn and a wave to Lucy. The larder refill would have to wait.

Samuel wrestled with his energy and tried to keep focused. He knew he had just taken a very dangerous corner far too fast and decided to slow down and catch his breath. He needed to see Gerard to put his mind at rest, but he mainly wanted to see his patients. He decided after the working day, which would be a late finish, around 9 PM he would have an early night, no matter what else would be asked of him.

Samuel found Doctor Gerard Bernstein in ward 8, he was checking three of the recovering patients. Samuel caught Gerard's eye and the two men found a quiet corner of ward 8 to transfer their information.

Gerard was delighted that Samuel had returned early as he was starting to realize what pressure he had placed on Samuel, being away from the hospital at such a needy time. Gerard also realized he had been consumed by his own worries long enough, so when Samuel apologized for not sorting out the larder refill, Gerard waved his hand in embarrassment.

"Sorry, Samuel, I have already asked far too much of you and not treated you as the professional doctor you are, kindly forgive me. I have indulged too long in my own sorrow during this worldwide pandemic, I am ashamed."

Lucy returned breathless to Brown's Donkey Sanctuary, she picked up the basket of carrots and headed down the field feeding the donkeys as she went. She welcomed the little donkeys as they greeted her and some cheeky ones helped themselves to a carrot, Lucy laughed as they appeared to smile mischievously.

Lucy could see Snowdrops at the bottom of the field, standing beside the stone wall that separated the donkeys from Mr. Hill's garden. She made her way to Snowdrops who was looking over the stone wall into the wild flowered garden. Lucy sat on the wall and looked into the garden, hoping to see Sally or Mr. Hill but there was no sign of anyone.

Sally's husband Johnny had returned to his ship several days before, so she wondered if Sally was on the telephone with him. She noticed some of the flowers looked so incredibly bright colored, especially two of the Daisies. Lucy blinked and queried her own eyesight.

The daisies were yellow with white petals, but that was all Lucy could accept as normal. They had wings in many shades of pink, and they were not only flying from flower to toadstools they were also hopping, and jumping, as if they were playing leapfrog or some similar game. Their legs and petal-like arms were green, and they had faces that were smiling directly at Lucy.

Horace sat on a rock, he had been sleeping under, but when he heard that Lucy was coming to visit Fairy Glen, he quickly crawled out, washed his face with a little damp grass, and sat on the rock. Fairy Snowbell and Tinkerbell arrived and flew to the top of a fox glove where they both sat with their legs dangling over the side.

"You are Fairies and Flower Fairies. Tell me please what do you want from me?" Lucy cried.

"Yes, we are two Miss Daisy Weed flower fairies, we told you about the retired racehorses. If we had not, they would have been returned and slaughtered, as it costs a lot to keep old and especially lame horses, and so we had to tell you."

"Just as now we have to inform you that one of the horses has a bad chest infection, he used to be called Holborn Boy. That is of the present, but it is of the not-too-distant future, we are to tell you of too, your knowledge Lucy, and your care and devotion will be needed for the animals."

"Some parts of the world are in a very bad state with climate changes, this affects not only humans and land, but innocent animals, that are already endangered species."

Seeing the concern and fear in Lucy's eyes, Tinkerbell decided she would explain. "You will not be alone; the Daisy flower fairies will never be far from you."

This, however, did not do anything to reassure poor Lucy, who had decided she was hallucinating and possibly quite mad. Snowbell decided to take a different approach. "Lucy, we have watched you grow into a lovely young lady, who seems to always want to help others."

Snowbell could see Lucy was starting to listen and appeared more relaxed. "We know you want to stay and help the donkey sanctuary, but Sally can manage for a while, also remember how you felt that you were missing out on friendships as you were not attending university."

Lucy agreed and decided to wait to hear all before jumping to conclusions. That would possibly be negative, based on fear. Snowbell could feel Lucy's thoughts stray to Doctor Samuel, and she looked directly into Lucy's eyes as she replied in a very soft tone. "Do not concern yourself over Doctor Samuel, he is thinking of traveling to third-world countries, as he wishes to help with vaccinations around the world, your paths will cross."

Lucy felt tired and wishing for her own familiar bedroom, walked away from what she believed was a dream, she found herself climbing the stone wall and running as fast as she could along the path at the back of the houses.

Lucy fled up the stairs two at a time and entered the bathroom. She turned the taps on and locked the door, but it was only her thoughts she was trying to lock out. She spotted Horace who was struggling to keep above the flow of water, Lucy grabbed the China soap dish and swooped him up, then placed him on the windowsill on a clean dry face cloth.

She began to sob, Oh Horace, don't you die, you are my faithful friend. Oh dear Horace, I must go away, the fairies have told me, where do I fear may be a very long way from here, and I don't want to go anywhere, and yet I do. Lucy cried louder and Horace smiled at Lucy, a smile that said all will be well, do not worry.

Lucy sank into the hot bubble bath that seemed to caress her very soul. She drifted off into the oblivion of cares but was quickly brought back to the moment by the telephone in her bedroom. As the answering machine switched on, she could hear a man's voice who she believed was Samuel.

Lucy took her time, enjoying the water which was starting to turn a little cold. She stepped out of the bath and glanced at Horace who appeared to be drying himself on the pink face cloth. "Come, Horace, let's go and listen to what Doctor Samuel has to say."

Lucy, now wrapped in a long fluffy pink dressing gown with the hood up and over her head walked calmly into the bedroom and picked up the phone. It was Doctor Samuel asking her to give him a quick ring when she was free. Lucy wondered had she forgotten to bolt the stables or feed the cats. "Hullo Doctor Samuel, Lucy here, is everything alright with the racehorses?"

"Oh sorry, Lucy, did I worry you, no it's not the Bernstein's residence, for a change."

Lucy giggled. "It's just I wondered do you fancy a quick drink tonight, well a bite to eat really, or whatever is your preference?"

"I would love a drink, as I feel I need one. You see, I have been talking to the fairies!"

"Then, my dear, I will pick you up in 30 minutes while your mind is still fresh and not blown away by the fairies."

It was a wonderful evening, with laughter and light conversation mixed with hot chocolate and brandy, which had been followed by a large red wine. A drive home and time to reflect on all the happenings of the past days. It was a clear night and a full moon, so when Samuel pulled into a country farm entrance, Lucy had no fears.

Samuel held Lucy in his arms and kissed her tenderly. Lucy had no hesitation and responded without doubts. They both sat back in the car seats, their heads close enough to hear each other's sighs and whispers of love.

Lucy lay awake, looking out of her bedroom window at the stars and thinking of Samuel. It all seemed a dream the whole night, and yet Lucy knew it was far from a dream and that she would see the fairies and flower fairies again, and also kiss Doctor Samuel once again.

Chapter 8
Out of Body Experiences

Lucy had no intentions of trying to understand what was happening to her. All she knew was it felt as though she had two lives. She was the same person in a world that felt as real as the world she had been born into.

Lucy had received a letter from a third-world country that was using donkeys to carry bricks and rubbles. The gentleman who wrote the letter was Sir Linden Handa, a man who had given his life to animals around the world who were in a state of becoming extinct or treated cruelly for their skins or horns, and worse.

He explained to take the donkeys away from their owners that so needed them, was as wrong as leaving them to work in pain and bad conditions. It was a short letter straight to the point, asking if Lucy would fly out next week, for six months to teach these owners of so many injured donkeys, how to take care of them and love them.

Although the letter was short, it reduced Lucy to a flood of tears. Lucy's mother had rushed into her daughter's bedroom and cradled the sad Lucy. "Who has upset you? Well, we will see about this, no one upsets my girl."

Lucy pulled away slightly from her mother's welcomed open arms to reach the letter lying on the bed. "Surely, Lucy, you are not considering going, are you?"

"Oh, mother, how can I refuse, the donkeys are suffering through lack of knowledge. I have that knowledge."

"Before you decide, please talk to Sir Arthur, he can explain the dangers as I am sure he will have traveled there at some time in his life!"

Lucy looked more carefully at her atlas on her bedroom window. West Africa seemed an awful long way from her mother so talking to Sir Arthur, she welcomed. "Where exactly, Lucy?"

Lucy handed Sir Arthur the letter. "Ghana."

"Yes, I did travel there in my forties. I guess it will be very different now. I must add they were lovely people."

"I would travel to see you, Lucy, or go out with you until you settle. Just let me know, what you decide. I do know if you do not do it you will be sad and regret all your life, it's a calling. What about Doctor Samuel, Lucy? You and he appear to have a closeness."

"He is going to work abroad in third-world countries to help and teach the relevance of vaccinations."

Alexis Louise looked into the empty coffee cup and sighed deeply. It was still dark outside so starting chores to block out the sudden departure of her daughter to Western Africa was not an option. She wondered why she had told her precious daughter Lucy to go and talk to Sir Arthur, about making the long journey, it all seemed rather as if she had given her blessing on leaving.

Sir Arthur had only recently discovered Lucy was his own flesh and blood, and yet there she was, holding out the reins to him. She wanted to ring Sir Arthur and scream at him, how dare he give her daughter permission and blessing to go to a country she knew so little about.

Alexis had woke at 4 AM feeling angry with herself for allowing Lucy to go, but several strong coffees later and brandy had moved her anger to Sir Arthur. She decided to go back to bed and resist the temptation to ring Sir Arthur, which she knew without any doubt she would regret. Alexis placed a new full cup of coffee, in her favorite bone China white mug, with the Lily of the Valley flower on the side.

This, she decided, would make her feel a lot better, as Lucy had bought her the mug as a reminder of Sally and Johnny's wedding. The China mugs, which were of very good quality had been Lucy's idea, to sell in the donkey sanctuary's shop. They had sold out within a week, as the villages loved the wedding and simply loved Sally and Johnny, and, of course, Lucy, who was the bridesmaid.

Alexis pulled the duvet up and tried to sleep but gave up the idea as she recalled how much caffeine she had consumed. She was desperate to hear Lucy's voice and wondered would she settle. She had heard from Lucy, there had been text messages as her journey took her to West Africa, Ghana, then a haste telephone call to tell her she had arrived and it appeared fascinating, the people so warm and friendly.

She also had said it was getting dark and she needed to rest so would ring her again when she awoke, but that was several days ago, or was it? Alexis decided it was not as long as she thought it was, so perhaps it would be today she would ring. She no sooner relaxed with the happy thought of her daughter's phone call, than the phone rang. Alexis rushed to the hall and grabbed the telephone.

"Your shopping will be delivered between 10.20 AM and 11.20 AM today."

Alexis placed the receiver down and wept. This was her way of handling disappointments, anger was definitely not her and Lucy was exactly the same, tears no anger. Alexis sat up in bed and drank her coffee, making a mental note to purchase a few extra packets of the tasty blend.

It was a very cold morning but so very bright, the shopping had been put neatly away, and so she decided to not sit and torment r herself waiting for a phone call, but instead to go for a brisk walk through the village.

Alexis decided to walk past the donkey sanctuary, she spotted Sally a little way up the field; she was talking to a very stubborn donkey who had decided straw hats were out. "Can I help, Sally?"

"No thank you, unless you can bring Lucy back. It's Snowball and because he cannot have Lucy to give him his treats, he will get rid of his straw hat!"

Alexis laughed and felt not just close to her daughter, but also felt she had something to tell her about, that would certainly make her laugh. Sir Arthur spotted Alexis from his upstairs window and resisted the temptation to wave. He felt cautious and did not want to do anything that may upset Alexis.

He felt she had been more than fair under the circumstances. After all, it had been only a short time since he had found out that Lucy was his daughter, and realized he was fortunate that Alexis had been so kind and understanding. He decided to ring her later. Perhaps by then, Lucy may have made contact. She had promised to let him know as soon as she could what she thought of the work involved.

Lucy awoke, but no, she was sleeping. "Who are you?" she asked, "and where am I?"

"Lucy, you are safe we need your help."

"It is a little donkey, some bad owner has placed a heavy old mattress on its back and sent it off down a busy road, the donkey is frail, no food no water in days, and it is so tired. The mattress is so heavy, please help."

"Where am I to go? Am I dreaming? Is this a dream?"

"It is similar to another dimension, as real as the world you know as real."

"Come." Lucy could see the poor little donkey almost stumbling, and vehicles missing it by fractions. Lucy ran as fast as she could, but it appeared she was too late, as she watched the frightened little donkey fall over. Lucy arrived at the scene, not knowing what to expect. The exhausted donkey appeared to have toppled into a deep ditch and landed on the mattress tied to its back.

Lucy untied the ropes and laid the mattress flat, making it more comfortable for the donkey to sleep on. Some springs were sticking through the old mattress, but not on the part the donkey rested on. A stranger handed her a bucket of water, and Lucy lifted the head of the donkey gently so it could drink.

Satisfied with the water and a crust of bread with some butter, the donkey returned to his sleep. Lucy asked these strangers who all seemed not really there, could she leave the donkey and return later to take it somewhere safe. Lucy woke in her unfamiliar bed, yawned, and sat upright; that was no dream, that was as real as this is, and screamed out loud.

Lucy screamed with fright as she looked down at the dark green duvet cover on her small wooden bed. It was not the donkey playing tricks on her mind, or the shock of where she was, or even the rather depressing bed that was placed in the corner of the small room.

What had given Lucy the fright of her life was two Miss Daisy Weed flower fairies sitting on a yellow cushion. The cushion was one of three, placed on the side of the bed up against the wall. The flower fairies were staring at Lucy and had not flinched at her loud scream instead they were smiling.

"What on earth do you want, are you real? In fact, what is real for I am starting to disbelieve my own existence, am I dead? did I die of the virus?"

The flower fairies giggled. "All real, the donkey, and definitely we are real! Feel if you do not believe us, just feel." They both giggled and handed Lucy a green petal arm.

"No, thank you, flower fairies, it's taken me long enough to accept that Horace, the spider, shares my bedroom at home, and my bath water!" She exclaimed, "I am certainly not ready for shaking petals with fairies, or am I, what do I know anymore." Lucy sobbed. "I want my mother."

"She wants you too, so the sooner you work and do all the little jobs that we little fairies cannot do, the quicker you are home, well if you want to be home, that is."

"What is that supposed to mean? I question that, of course, I want to be home. This is all mind-blowing."

"Oh, Lucy, surely you want to take a carrot to that lovely tired little donkey, who is still in the ditch struggling to stand up. Oh and don't you want to find out its bad owner that sent him down such a busy road with the dirty heavy mattress tied tightly to his back."

"Yes, and yes, where do I go to find out where I was taken last night?"

"We know, we will take you. However, Lucy, we will have to hide on you, as you cannot fly, and you are too heavy for our pretty wings."

They giggled loudly and Lucy, who was craving a strong coffee, lost her patience. "Well, surprise, surprise, I never knew I had no wings, huh! Now go, I need coffee and a shower."

"We will just sit here and wait. Can you splash some cold water on us please we are starting to wilt with the heat?"

Lucy ignored their request and headed to the kitchen, where two young African boys were having coffee and toast. They spoke in French, explaining they had arrived from Guinea three weeks ago. They smiled at Lucy and offered Lucy coffee and food. Lucy returned to her room, sat on the bed and drank the delicious coffee.

Suddenly feeling brighter and far more alive, showered and dressed in cool shorts and a matching gray top. She then went back to the kitchen, filled a tumbler of cold water and returned to her room to find the two flower fairies delighted with the tumbler of cool water. They splashed and splashed, throwing water at each other. Lucy felt so guilty, as she had almost ignored their request.

"Lucy, can you get water and carrots for the donkey in the ditch, please."

"Yes, but I have barely been here five minutes and I don't want to abuse the opportunity of my post by disappearing."

"Do not worry, Lucy, we can make all that part just perfect." They were smiling from petal to petal.

Lucy started to smile back, "Oh your clever little flower fairies, it's all magic."

"OK, let's go." Lucy could feel her mobile, in her rucksack vibrating, and guessed it would be her mother, who would be concerned, yet Lucy had no intentions of holding up this mission a moment longer.

Lucy returned to a field with lots of ill and injured donkeys, where she had been taken on arrival. She quickly found one of the teams helping the donkeys, and explained, that she needed to rescue a very distressed little donkey stuck in a hedge. A lift was offered on the back of a bicycle and Lucy pointed to a major road.

The young man cycled off with Lucy, who wished she had her own lilac bike. Lucy pointed to where some branches of a hedgerow seemed to have fallen over the path at the side of the busy road, and the poor little injured donkey lay exhausted after a struggle to rid itself of the mattress. Lucy had untied it but the donkey had no energy left.

"We will go and talk to him, and tell him not to worry, all will be well." The two flower fairies whispered into Lucy's ear in unison.

The young boy stood holding his bike and asked, "How do we get this little fellow back to the sanctuary, he is surely dying."

Lucy produced the liter bottle of water and carrots from her rucksack and proceeded to stroke and pat the donkey. An old broken China basin was used to give the donkey a drink, and what was left Lucy used to bathe its sores. The donkey responded although he was too weak to eat, he sniffed the carrots. Lucy tied the rope around its neck very gently.

The donkey loved the flower fairies that were sitting on each of his ears, tickling him. "Come on, we are going to sit here with you all the way back to a rather nice field where you can have more water and eat those juicy carrots when you decide to."

The donkey tried and tried to stand, but when the young boy came over the donkey seemed to respond, Lucy held the front of the donkey while the young man, called Jamil placed the donkeys back legs in a better and easier position for it to stand. Jamil obviously had learned lots about these adorable animals, she could not wait to hear how he knew so much.

The donkey walked between Lucy and Jamil all the way back up the bank to the donkey field. He drank more water and eventually ate two carrots. It was the start of his recovery and with tears in her eyes, she thanked the young man. "It's fine, lady, we all who work here love the donkeys, just as you do, but how did you know the donkey was there in the ditch?"

That was a question that Lucy never answered, instead she walked around the donkeys in the field to see what she could do for them. There were a few with chest problems, possibly the dust they had worked under. The little donkey they named Tiny.

Chapter 9
Time Passengers

Lucy hurried back to her lodgings and fled up the stairs to her room. She quickly showered and got under her duvet. She felt she had reached her breaking point and did not want a call from the Manager or any member of the team, asking her to check some injured donkey. Lucy did not want to be disturbed by the flower fairies, she wanted peace and normality. She decided if she had a television set, she would kiss it.

She got out of bed and locked her bedroom door. She returned to bed determined to escape these busy nights with the flower fairies and busy days with the team workers, who worked endlessly helping the donkeys. Two Daisy flower fairies flew over her head, and she screamed at them, scaring them half to death. "Go away, let me sleep. Can you not even give me one night to sleep?"

"Yes, Lucy, you never have to tell us or in fact, any fairy how you feel, we already know."

"Then why are you here keeping me awake?"

"We came to give you good news about Doctor Samuel."

"Oh, then flower fairies, I am very sorry, what news do you have?"

"We believe he is at present traveling to see you. He wrote to you several weeks ago, but a lot of mail appears to get lost in transit or just takes a very long time." They yawned in unison and closed their eyes.

Lucy rushed to the kitchen to get a tumbler of fresh water and cursed the fact she had locked the bedroom door. She rushed back to find the flower fairies starting to turn brown on their white petals. She gently splashed them thoroughly with the cool water but they appeared to be dying as they were definitely drying out.

Lucy found some cotton wool which she dipped into the water, then began to stroke the Daisies, gently turning them to do the backs of their petals. She was tempted to place them in the water but resisted as she feared they would float or drown, which was too big a risk to take. Suddenly, Fairy Snowbell and Tinkerbell flew into the bedroom and swooped the dying flower fairies up.

Lucy returned to her bed in deep thought. Doctor Samuel traveling, Daisy flower fairies, and must ring my mother, also Judge Arthur. Lucy wondered what was happening. She knew it was all real, as since Tiny the donkey had been rescued, the flower fairies had engineered several rescues of mules, donkeys, and working horses.

She had always used the sanctuary the following day to take overworked and abused animals. Jamil continued to ask the question, but how did you know? The dark circles under Lucy's eyes convinced Jamil that Lucy must walk the streets at night looking for these injured animals.

He adored Lucy for her dedication, and this inspired him to walk some streets at night also but with little success. He too had dark lines under his eyes.

Lucy did not ring her mother or Judge Arthur. Instead, she lay on her bed, a sheet pulled over her, and slept soundly. The dream was very busy, and something felt urgent. Fairies were calling her name and pointing with their wands and asking her to follow quickly. A forest with flames that seemed to touch the sky was shown to her.

Lucy reminded herself she was dreaming, that this was not really happening, and yet the heat was scorching her bare legs and arms. She held her hand over her face to protect herself, but the heat was so intense she had to try to escape it, but how, where to run to?

She felt the flames all around her and dropped to the ground beside a large tree that seemed to be surviving the flames. She could hear the tree crying. She moved closer to it and placed her arms around the massive trunk. "Do not cry, you will be fine. You are a red bark tree, and your creator designed you to withstand heat and flames, although this is a bit too much of a test."

Lucy remembered the books she had read so long ago, it felt like a lifetime, in the village library when she was looking at what insects and spiders were living on the barks of unusual trees. "Your bark is sponge-like, so plenty of moisture to protect you."

At that, the fire appeared to stop trying to ignite this magnificent red bark and appeared to retreat. Lucy could feel cooler air, which appeared to be coming from the roots of the tree, and a breeze blew down from the top of the highest branches. The tree thanked Lucy for her knowledge and bowed his branches as she vanished out of sight.

Lucy turned over onto her side, but her side was as sore as her legs and arms. She got out of bed and went to the kitchen, not knowing whether or not it was morning or still night. Jamil looked with horror at Lucy. "Where on earth did you walk to last night, you are black and bleeding."

Lucy looked down at her burned legs and replied with total honesty, "I really don't know, the trees."

Lucy never finished her sentence, as she gasped and held her hand out to Jamil, who rushed to her side and guided her to a chair. Lucy yelped like an injured animal when she tried to sit, "I am burned, please help me, Jamil."

Jamil rushed out of the kitchen leaving Lucy amazed at his actions, until she heard him calling back to her. "Please wait I have a doctor Samuel who is wishing to see you. That is why I was in the kitchen, waiting to tell you."

Doctor Samuel ran behind Jamil, listening to his garbled conversation. "She is badly burned by trees," was all Samuel could make out.

Lucy was a total mystery to Samuel, so he did not ask Jamil to explain. Jamil was pleased not to try to explain as this may involve Lucy's Street walking at night, and Jamil did not want Lucy to stop that as they had rescued hundreds of injured and abused animals since Lucy arrived.

However, he was quite confused hearing news that there were trees burning and felt sure he would have heard something if there had been a forest fire. He pointed to where the door was leading to Lucy's lodgings and Doctor Samuel rushed in and up the narrow stairs which led to the kitchen, and Lucy who sat crying with pain on the chair Jamil had sat her in not knowing how badly burned she was.

Samuel carried Lucy gently back to her bedroom and lay her on her bed. "I need to examine your burns. Lucy. Is that alright or do you prefer me to take you to the hospital, where they have all the correct medication for such burns? You also may need to be sedated, do you understand?"

Lucy's reply was not what Samuel expected, but he understood she meant every word. "I will be fine, just cold water and let me sleep."

Samuel only left Lucy's side twice while she slept soundly, once to get a coffee and second to read a paper where no fires were mentioned. Lucy felt drowned in fairy healing drops and listened as Snowbell explained that she should have waited for the Flower fairies to return and take her, as they know the Amazon and the fires that appear to happen more often than ever before.

Snowbell bathed Lucy's legs and arms and placed a special fairy ointment made only under a full moon, on her face and hands.

Samuel knew what he had seen, although he also knew no one on planet earth would believe him, well the fairies would, he thought, and smiled.

He had seen the white sheet covering Lucy lift up into the air and a rather beautiful angel or fairy, or both, pour a special liquid on her wand, which was waved over Lucy's body.

Lucy awoke and held out her hands, and this adorable fairy swooped gracefully in and out of Lucy's hands, and at the same time, a cloud of strong-smelling cherry blossom drafted in the air, then landed on Lucy's face. Samuel watched as the fairy flew out of the bedroom window. Lucy, her eyes closed, was back in a deep sleep.

Chapter 10
On Strike

"Why are you resting, sweet little Flower fairies, when there is such a lot to do?"

Horace was pleased with what he had said, as he could tell he was getting a reaction from them. Horace could not wait to tell them his delightful news and thought the best way to wake them and get a quick response was to say something that would provoke them. He knew they almost died of dehydration, and that they had traveled far doing good deeds, which had pleased the fairies.

Horace waited patiently as the Flower fairies rubbed their tired eyes with their rather dried petals. "It's alright, tired Flower fairies, Horace is not on your good deed list, so just sleep, my news regarding my clever son can wait, perhaps I am not important enough but that's alright just sleep."

Horace turned to walk away, then quickly turned back just in time to see the two Miss Daisy Weed flower fairies fall fast asleep. Horace realizing this time he had gone too far to make the Flower fairies feel guilty, picked a rather large leaf for a spider to carry, and struggled over to where the flower fairies lay struggling to live, he placed the leaf wet with morning dew, over them leaving only their faces showing.

As he walked back to where his mother rested in her new conservatory, she had heard her son and had also watched with tears in her eyes as she saw him place the leaf. This emotional action appeared to have been viewed by quite a few fairies and also Lily in the Lily Pond.

Fairy Tinkerbell and Snowbell flew to Horace and asked. "What is it, Horace? Do you have some news to share with us?"

"Oh yes, kind fairies, I have good and bad news. What would you like first?"

"We would like good news first. We all need to be cheered up as I fear we are all heartbroken, as our Flower fairies may not recover. We all love them so very much, and we also know you love them too."

Horace answered honestly, "They light up my life, but you see, it's Lucy I love even more, or I think more, perhaps just different. Lucy has always needed me, whereas the Flower fairies have each other, and do not need me."

"Oh, dear Horace, we all need each other in different ways. Come now, what is your good news?"

"It's my clever son. As you may recall, he had lots of spiderlings and had not taken his responsibilities to care for them. My mother, his grandmother brought them all up, and I have a feeling there may be more for his grandmother to bring up. He does not appear to learn, and worse neither does the mother of all these rather attractive spiderlings."

"She told me she cannot live with him, Horace 2, that is, and cannot live without him. My poor mother is in the autumn of her life and the corner of the shed where she lives had a hole, making it very drafty, and this, little kind fairies, is where the good news is."

Horace seemed to compose himself, ready to give the good news. "My clever son realizing the extent of the problem of the hole, and draft causing his grandmother severe pain in her legs, with her bad arthritis, completely solved the problem. For quite a long time, on the other side of the hole in the corner of the shed, was a rose tree planted by Mr. Hill, a red rose tree."

"My clever son used the rose tree and made a spider's web covering some branches, using its stem as a main support, the shape of this web, in my whole spider life, I have never seen before. You see little fairies, my son has made with his webs for his grandmother, a conservatory."

The fairies smiled with happiness and congratulated Horace on his son's achievement.

"When it is sunny, my mother comes out of the hole, which is not at all drafty now, and bathes in the warmth of the sun. He is a genius, just like his father, and his father before!"

"Now, Horace, the bad news, but tell us quickly as we can see the two Daisy flower fairies are waking."

"I was lying under my own mossy rock when one of the working bees landed, he was so annoyed and appeared to be talking to himself, he said many times, I am on strike, buzzzzzz strike buzzzzz, strrrr buzzzzzz. I believe he is not on his own as I have seen and heard many working bees buzzing the same word, 'strike', they do not sound at all happy with their decision, almost as if they have been forced to make it."

Horace felt the conversation far too serious and decided he was going to wait for the Flower fairies to wake up and hopefully have a more cheerful chat with them, and yet he knew he had done right informing the fairies that the working bees were on strike. Horace heard the Flower fairies speaking Lucy's name and quickly crawled to where he could hear clearer.

Fairy Snowbell was comforting the Flower fairies and telling them to rest and recover. "No no please, Lucy is so tired and working night and day. Please help her or let us return."

"You are so weak, as it was really far too hot for a daisy and oh so tasking for you, not forgetting the long journey, rest and recover, then let us talk."

Tinkerbell and Snowbell flew off before the Flower fairies could reply. Fairies do not argue, they just think and say good, then leave. The Flower fairies turned over to allow the petals they had been sleeping on to recover and were about to fall asleep when Horace arrived.

"Good day, little Flower fairies, who have possibly missed poor troubled Horace, who is extremely proud of his son who has just built a conservatory for his grandmother."

He turned hesitantly to crawl away and then waited for the response he knew he would get. "Then why are you troubled? Do you not like the conservatory?"

"Kind Flower fairies, can you fly me to where Lucy is? For I fear she may be crying, and I need to comfort her. Could you take me tonight, or should I wait for her in her bedroom?"

"No, Horace, this is not possible as we do not know where Lucy is or how to get to her."

Horace was shocked as he heard them lie, or so he thought. "Flower fairies, you have been with Lucy. How could you lie to poor Horace." Horace decided perhaps he did not love these Flower fairies after all. It's alright little Flower fairies, I will just crawl under a rock and think of how you could lie. The Flower fairies were so weak they could not lift their petals to answer Horace and fell promptly asleep.

Doctor Samuel left Lucy's side and drove at speed to the general hospital where he was about to start work. He somehow knew that Lucy was fine and that the next time he saw her, she would be completely recovered. He also knew he would keep everything he had witnessed to himself. He decided without a second thought that a medical doctor believing in fairies was not a strong point to have.

He smiled to himself and thought a UFO would be easier to explain. Surely, this was equally as hard for Lucy to come to terms with. He would arrange to take Lucy out to dinner on the coming Friday and see where the conversation would lead, perhaps she would have no recollection of the fairies, yet he remembered how she had mentioned the fairies previously.

The two Daisy flower fairies woke at the same time, they felt weak but somehow knew they were starting to recover. Horace crawled out from under his rock and stared at the two flower fairies who had just lied to him. "Why, little Flower fairies, could you lie to poor harmless Horace who can barely walk, and has an elderly mother to look after, but it's alright little good deed flower fairies, Horace is low down your good deed list!"

"What are you talking about, Horace?"

"I just asked you where Lucy was and—" Poor Horace did not finish his sentence, as a very angry working bee had flown into him knocking him clean into the air. Horace landed on his back and struggled to get upright.

"How dare you take your anger out on a harmless spider, what is wrong with you, have you not collected enough pollen or nectar, I think you owe Horace an apology, and also you could explain your anger to us."

Horace was delighted that the Flower fairies had spoken up for him and quickly decided they were his very best friends, after Lucy. "Buzz, strike, strike not right Queen Bee gets bzzzzz."

Horace crawled back to the Flower fairies as the angry bee flew over their heads. "They are on strike, all the working bees, as Queen Bee, their mother, promised they would be Queen Bee one day."

"So why Horace are they angry about being Queen Bee one day?" Horace gave his best smile knowing he had the Flower fairies' attention at last.

"It's just that Queen Bee says that to all her many daughters, who are all her working bees." Horace continued with the wonderful interesting information he had heard while sitting in his mother's new conservatory, "Queen Bee chose one of the Drones to have her babies too, but she chose the boyfriend of the angry bee you have just witnessed, her own daughter's boyfriend."

"Oh goodness, so she has lied to all her daughters, or perhaps she does not know herself who will be Queen, as she will be replaced one day when she cannot carry out her duties." Horace sat quietly listening and learning.

"Surely it is tradition, and possibly as Queen Bee she needs to talk to them all, as I am sure having babies after babies cannot be so wonderful a position to be in, sounds like quite a commitment, that gives her very little time for pleasure."

A small working bee who was also on strike had never looked at her mother's important position in quite the same way as the Flower fairies had explained. She flew out of the blades of grass and circled Horace and the Flower fairies. "Thankzzzbuzzzzwillzzzbuzzzexplainzzzz."

Fairy Snowbell had also listened to the kind of explanation from the Flower fairies and wondered if it was the right time to give them even more problems to sort out.

"If you feel rested enough to help with another problem." The Flower fairies felt that to be honest, their reply should be yes, and yet they so wanted to rest longer. "It should not take too long it is to do with Princess Precious Hairdressing shop."

Fairy Snowbell paused and began to eat a black cherry. She nimbly nibbled around the stone, and then carefully placed the stone in a small basket to dry in the sun. There were many different stones from various fruits already in the basket, awaiting the right full moon to plant them into the ground.

Fairies needed a continuous supply of fruit, so all stones were kept and planted by special fairies, who had magic hands. The fairies that had special magic hands traveled the world planting and nurturing fruit trees. They often stayed in the hot countries where the vines needed lots of important help, as often they caught infections.

They were always the happiest fairies, with names appropriate to their work, Fairy Cherrybell was a little plump and always eating her cherries she was loved by all fairies so when she arrived on the chosen full moon, all the fairies in Fairy Glen rejoiced. The fruit trees all grew so fast and Cherrybell got all the praise for the good season of fruit.

Fairy Snowbell continued and explained, "It is something to do with the red beetroot juice Princess Precious uses for dyeing hair, mainly gray squirrel's hair. In fact, the hairdressing shop appears to be more known as Hare dressing shop."

"I would prefer you to leave immediately and return before the sun starts to go down." There was another long pause and Snowbell coughed quietly, then explained she had a sore throat and that she also needed sleep to heal. "I will have fresh turned upright mushrooms ready for your rest when you return, and two very tall fox gloves for your morning fresh dew."

"Please leave now, I will follow all your thoughts. Go in peace, little Miss Daisy Flower fairies, for that is who you are, peacemakers."

Chapter 11
Peace

"Peace, peace you say." Cecil shook his head and walked in circles on his hind legs around the two Miss Daisy Weeds. "Yes, Cecil, we bring peace as we are peace Flower fairies, sent to you by fairy Snowbell."

They stood waiting for a reply from Cecil but received in true rabbit form, the word peace being repeated. Cecil was agitated, angry and impatient. "It's a rabbit step too far this time."

He paused for quite a while as if he was not remembering what he was annoyed about. Cecil remembered, stopped circling, and lent up against a strong tree root that had successfully broken through the roof of the burrow a short while ago.

"It's a group of bad rabbits, bad I say, bad, that I have brought up single-handed, and this is all the rabbit thanks I get." Cecil made a loud screeching noise and fell to the ground weeping. "They have all stolen, stolen, I say, my ideas and the red beetroot hair dye."

"Now Princess Precious and I will starve and not be able to manage. All my children, yes, my children will starve."

"Cecil, why are they stealing your ideas?"

Cecil let go of the tree root and looked frustrated with the question. "It's acorns in the burrow, burrow I say my good idea, and they, the bad rabbits, which I fear maybe my children are using the red dye that we have emptied into the small stream. Princess Precious heard some of the bad rabbits calling out in the forest to the gray squirrels to come and bathe in the red dye for half an acorn each."

"Half an acorn, Cecil, how do they half the acorn?" The flower fairies were genuinely interested.

"Teeth, teeth, with their teeth."

They could not conceal their giggles any longer and decided this silly situation deserved a quick solution. "Cecil, if the bad rabbits are your children, then they are a chip off the old block, very enterprising just like you."

Cecil, who had commenced circling once again, stopped suddenly and stared at the two Daisy flower fairies as if he was seeing them for the first time. "It's a compliment, Cecil, and it saves wasting the beetroot dye." They paused just long enough for Cecil to blink, then continued. "Perhaps you make a new sign with Cecil and Sons Hairdressing, maybe you give them your fatherly blessing."

Cecil was delighted, and turned to leave without a farewell, when suddenly he stopped and turned around, and shrieked, peace, peace, peace.

Their return to Fairy Glen was difficult to remember and as they lay welcoming their sleep and dreams, the two flower fairies turned to face each other and smiled, a smile that was close to a giggle that had not sleep been waiting.

Lucy had totally recovered after a few nights of deep sleep. She worked hard all day with the injured and traumatized donkeys and horses. She loved her job and decided she needed far more studying both in theory and practice. The opportunity arose the very next day as she tried to hold an injured donkey still while she bandaged its sores.

A local vet arrived, he had lived in many different countries, always looking to help these incredible, clever, and forgiving donkeys. Eugene was from Spain and was possibly the most inspiring man she had ever met. He was so knowledgeable both about the health of the animals, but also about the government rules. He had personally transported hundreds of retired or badly injured donkeys to various sanctuaries around the world.

He had heard of Brown's Donkey Sanctuary, previously Hill's Sanctuary, and decided there and then he would not only visit Lucy's home and Brown's Sanctuary but that if acceptable by Sally and Johnny Brown, deliver at least fifty of these older and retired donkeys.

"I can give them medical care, but they need affection and love, which I have no time to give." Lucy smiled tears in her eyes at the solution presented to her by this dedicated man who had given his life and certainly his youth, to these animals.

Samuel could hardly wait for the evening, he had worked hard at the hospital and felt his heart was breaking not just from lack of seeing Lucy, but over the small children he was treating. Some had caught the virus, but others suffered similar ailments to what he had seen at his last hospital.

Samuel waited patiently in his car outside a rather swish restaurant that had decking outside leading to a tree house.

Lucy insisted she would meet him there as she knew if she stayed too long at her lodgings, she would get drawn into more donkey work. She already felt guilty leaving the animals when there appeared to be still so much work to do.

She quickly showered and changed and decided to stop at a rather nice dress shop she had spotted the first week she had arrived. On leaving the shop, Lucy looked transformed from her green overalls and white shirt and wore a pale pink cotton knee-length dress, matching shawl, and white flat sandals. Lipstick was applied as an afterthought and perfume being her love was applied generously.

Samuel blinked in disbelief and quickly got out of the car to greet Lucy, who looked amazing. He was used to seeing Lucy in her work clothes, usually covered in mud, and had almost forgotten how wonderful she could look. His arms uncontrollably wrapped around her and as he pulled her gently close to him, he bent down and kissed her tenderly on her lips. The kiss seemed almost impossible to stop and it took a lot of willpower from Samuel to release his lips from hers. "I love you," he whispered.

Lucy neither hearing the traffic nor the music coming from the bar, reached up on her toes and as Samuel bent his head once again and answered her responding lips, "I love you too, my darling Samuel, who can we tell, for I am bursting to tell someone. Shall we tell the donkeys first, my love?"

Originally, they had both felt hungry, as both had rushed from work without thought of food, but suddenly all they were now hungry for was each other's love. Although it was a very warm evening, it helped them both to relax from all their worries and cares that awaited them.

Although Lucy had completed a lot of work at the sanctuary, she felt she was going at her own pace and not torn from such needed sleep by two Flower fairies. Lucy wondered how much she should tell Samuel. Should she tell him of her dreams that she knew were not dreams but reality, like two worlds, the world she knew and now another world that was every bit as real? How do you explain something you cannot comprehend or find an explanation for?

Yet these dreams guided Lucy giving her an insight into where donkeys and horses were in harm's way, also showing her treatments to help and cure the injured or infirmed animals. She was asked many times by Jamil, "How did you know where they were to be found, or what was wrong with them?"

The treatment Lucy applied to the animals; Jamil believed she must have been taught at university. Lucy prayed hard to the Almighty that the gifts she had been given would only be used in the way they had been given for.

Samuel took a good drink from his glass of whiskey and soda and was about to mention the little fairy that was so busy dabbing some special fairy ointment on Lucy's badly burned skin.

Samuel gasped as his eyes drifted over Lucy's perfect skin where not a trace of any burn was showing. He decided to finish the remainder of the whiskey in his glass, head to the bar for a refill, and not mention the little fairy. Perhaps he had just been very tired or perhaps the heat was affecting him, yet rather than thinking up what he certainly did not believe in, he decided to leave the matter until a far more suitable time.

Lucy and Samuel may have held back what they could not explain, but their love for each other had no boundaries. When a very happy smiling waiter offered them a job in his now-empty bar, they knew it was time to leave. Feeling so relaxed and happy, they both laughed back at the waiter, who knew love was certainly in the air.

Samuel decided to leave his car parked where it was and walk Lucy back along the narrow, still very busy streets, to her residence. They were beckoned by another friendly waiter who spotted the happy couple smiling, arms around each other. "Come be my guests. I have hot coffee and cognac."

It had been a magical night, true to what this couple had experienced since they had first met each other, now so long ago, or so it seemed.

"Marry me, Lucy, for I know there is no one else for me but you Lucy." Samuel waited for a reply and then smiled and looked deep into Lucy's eyes. "For I do believe, my dear, we are both away with the fairies."

Chapter 12
Home Is Where the Heart Is

Sally sat on the front of the tractor at the very top of the donkey sanctuary field. When she heard her mobile ringing the first few notes from her favorite piano concerto, thinking it was her husband Johnny, who was due to arrive around noon, she answered, "Hullo darling, where are you?"

"Er Sally, it's me, Lucy. Can you talk please? Just five minutes, I promise."

"Lucy, how wonderful to hear your voice. I thought it was Johnny as his ship docked early morning. Tell me, what is it, Lucy?"

"It is Samuel. He has asked me to marry him, and I wanted you to be the first to know."

"Did you say yes?"

"No, not yet, as I am young and feel I have lots to do with my life, and yet I want to say yes, as I love him so very much, and the thoughts of losing him, well I cannot bear to think about that."

There was a pause, then Sally spoke very slowly and calmly. "I felt very similar, I think we both did a bit as we were both young and had lots to do with our life and yet I have no regrets, I love Johnny more and more each day that passes.”

“I have a feeling it will be the same for you. There is no substitute for love.” Sally paused and then spoke again, “It makes a hard-working day a wonderful day, even if you’re freezing cold, covered in mud, ten fences to mend, and a tractor broken.” The two girls giggle and said their farewells.

“Samuel, can you talk for just a minute, please?”

“My darling Lucy, how good to hear you. What is it? Have I tired you out too much with our wonderful evening?”

“Samuel, my answer is yes.”

The phone had gone dead, and Lucy decided to make her way to work, along the dusty track leading up to the donkey sanctuary. She could see Eugene in the distance with a few donkeys standing close by. As she got closer, she called out to him a cheerful good morning and headed over to see if she could help him in any way. The donkey Eugene was struggling to hold steady was a new arrival.

“He has glass in his leg, must have lain down on it, and also a very bad whelp, which I fear has been given by a very angry owner, who discovered his donkey was unable to work. This is an old donkey, and the owner must have had many working years out of him, dreadful to treat such a loyal animal like this.” Eugene wiped a tear from his eye.

“Well, that is that this donkey is not working a second longer. He is for Brown’s Sanctuary.” Lucy smiled, “Yes indeed, he is so lovely.” Lucy placed her arms gently around the chestnut-haired donkey's neck and kissed him tenderly on the nose.

"Can I have one of those kisses, please?" Lucy spun around to face where the voice had come from. Samuel, his face beaming, walked over to Lucy and kneeled at her feet. "Lucy, my love, will you marry me?"

"Yes, Samuel, I would love to."

Samuel sat in his car outside of Lucy's lodgings, his heart pounded with excitement, and although he had seen Lucy at the donkey sanctuary early morning and rejoiced with her acceptance of marriage. He had to leave immediately as his hospital had called, a child had been rushed in by ambulance with breathing problems.

So it felt like a lifetime waiting to end his shift, he also knew Lucy had to travel to the next town with Eugene to help with a very stubborn donkey that was holding up the traffic. Samuel just wanted to run up the stairs and hammer on Lucy's door, but he knew that was not what Lucy expected of him, and so he sat patiently waiting.

Lucy had not long arrived back, it had been a very difficult afternoon, the owner of the stubborn donkey threatening to kill the donkey if they did not buy it. Eugene argued back to no avail and so an amount was agreed and a very stubborn donkey trotted off with Lucy. Lucy loved this very clever little gray and white donkey and called it Grayspots.

Lucy could see Samuel sitting in his car and after a hot shower quickly pulled on a cream cotton top with lace around the top and white smart-fitting trousers, pink sandals, and a pink messenger bag. Inside the bag, she had placed all her documents, passport, birth certificate, driving license, and some medical papers.

Like Samuel, she was desperate to see him and as she slid graciously into the passenger seat, it felt like electricity was binding them.

"The power of love," Samuel whispered.

They drove to the restaurant where the night before the waiter had called out to them to have a nightcap of coffee and cognac, he had not charged them, and although Samuel insisted, the waiter whose father they found out owned the magnificent restaurant, would not change his mind. They thanked him and told the waiter called Anwar they would return soon.

As they walked hand in hand through a white arch leading to the bar of the restaurant, Anwar rushed out to greet them. "Come, my friends, let me find you the best table in the house, but first let me get you a cool drink."

Anwar eyed the couple up and down, they were both so handsome and stood out in the crowd, but it was something else that Anwar saw and felt in their faces. "You are both so in love. Come, tell me, a little about your romantic life."

They both laughed, and Lucy spoke first. "I work with donkeys and horses, and today a very stubborn donkey."

Anwar laughed and looked at Samuel. "Oh well, let's see today I had a little girl with a virus and a little boy with breathing problems." Samuel looked down at his shoes and swallowed as he thought of the two children who might not make it through the night.

"No, please, Sir, don't let me make you sad, you are my happiest customers, we must not empty my restaurant, or I will have to drag more customers off the streets, or my father may beat me."

They all laughed and drank gratefully the red wine. Lucy could not wait, she had to tell someone and although Sally knew, she needed someone where she was to know. "We are getting married."

Anwar threw his hands up and clapped loudly. "Oh, how wonderful, my friends. When is the big day?"

Samuel looked at Lucy and smiled. "Anwar, it cannot be soon enough for me, but Lucy and I have not discussed the date yet, as we have just decided to get married."

"Then let me help you. Would you like to get married here, right here say in a few days' time, think about it and let me know."

To Samuel's surprise, Lucy reached out and held his hand firmly, and said, "I would love to."

Samuel gasped with delight and shock. "Then Anwar, what do we do? Do you need our documents to copy as I have mine with me?"

"I also have mine," Lucy said opening her bag.

Samuel and Lucy sat almost in a trance thinking of what they were doing, firstly handing all their documents over to a man they hardly knew, yet somehow, they trusted Anwar, and even more crazy was getting married in a week's time, but this was a lovely kind of crazy, never to be forgotten.

It was a very different night from the one before. They sat quietly, yet both were thinking exactly the same. How would their marriage affect their lives? What if one wanted to work in another country, or return home to the United Kingdom? Surely, they would both want to do various different things.

Samuel spoke first. "Lucy, we can compromise. We don't have to always agree. Surely, we are adult enough to understand if one of us wants to work somewhere different."

"Yes, Samuel, I agree and yet the way I feel, you are my home, so wherever we are, I am home. I guess its true home is where the heart is."

The doubts disappeared and the two held each other's hand so tightly, never to let go of their love for each other. "Come, Lucy, let's have some champagne and celebrate."

Samuel had barely finished his sentence when Anwar, true to form, presented them with a very large bottle of pink champagne. Anwar seemed almost as happy as they were, and as the champagne flowed, the conversation did also. Samuel decided to give Lucy a rough idea of his plans for the future.

"I want to work in Spain for a while and do a little more studying, as I enjoy working with children and need to have far more knowledge than what I have, perhaps we could consider that in a few years, at present we are new here and learning, so maybe we will both be ready for a move by then, if not, we will work out what fits us both and where is best to live, what I can assure you of, Lucy, is I do not ever want to be anywhere you are not."

Lucy felt a weight had been lifted and suddenly she felt excited at the thoughts of being Samuel's wife. "We need to go shopping for rings, although I fear we will not always be able to wear them in the professions we are both in, perhaps we also buy chains so that we can also wear them around our necks."

Lucy giggled at Samuel who appeared to be perhaps overthinking the rings. "We had best tell my mother and Judge Arthur."

It was only then that Lucy realized she knew so little about Samuel; she had never wanted to ask questions but now suddenly it felt wrong that she had not.

Lucy wanted her wedding to be quiet and meaningful, but what to wear was not as easy a decision as she had first thought. She looked at the dresses she had brought, and they were far from appropriate, and although she had convinced herself of just choosing a pretty dress, something deep inside told her that one day she would regret not having made a bigger effort.

Walking down the narrow streets to where she had discovered the dress shop seemed a good start. As she entered the shop, the lady who had served her just a short while ago came over to her. "So lovely to see you again. I do hope the dress lived up to your expectations."

Lucy giggled and hugged the shocked lady. "It most certainly did and now I am engaged to be married in a week's time, which is why I am here, as once again I desperately need your help."

"Oh my dear, how wonderful!" The lady beamed at Lucy, who felt so happy she could burst. "The problem is we do not sell wedding gowns; however, I may have something very appropriate."

"Can you call back tomorrow evening to see what you think of it? I do know it will fit, it's just would you wear it." Lucy left the shop totally confused and decided not to dwell on it but instead ring her mother.

"You are going to do what? Have you lost your mind, Lucy? You barely know Samuel."

The conversation did not improve and when her mother put the receiver down, Lucy was in tears and in no fit state to ring Sir Judge Arthur. Alexis looked with disbelief at the telephone, she had been expecting a call from her daughter to apologize for her lack of ringing, instead she was talking about getting married. She poured a rather large cognac and rang Judge Arthur.

"She is getting married. I mean, Lucy is getting married, our daughter. Are you there Arthur? Can you hear what I am saying, getting married to Doctor Samuel?"

Sir Arthur rarely got phased but hearing Alexis's sob, and thinking of Lucy all those miles away, he suddenly did feel rather angry. What on earth would make someone so independent as Lucy want to get married so quickly? She was young and brilliant; he decided to withhold judgment until he had spoken directly to Lucy.

Lucy had gulped a glass of red malbec and decided to ring her friend, Sally. She was sitting outside of a very small but quaint bar that the locals seemed to be at home in. Sally was delighted to hear from Lucy. "Have you some good news, Lucy? Is Samuel with you?"

"Yes, I have good news. I am getting married to Samuel next week, just a small, dignified wedding."

"Hullo, Sally, are you still there?"

"Yes, Lucy, just picking myself off the floor. I am delighted, Lucy, he is perfect for you, and when you know, you know. You are young but I was too when I married Johnny, and I am so happy, and you will be too. Oh, and do not listen to anyone, it is your life!"

"Wow!" was all Lucy could answer, and at that she thanked her best friend and headed home, feeling at peace with her wedding plans.

Alexis sat on the sofa beside Sir Arthur and wished she had not had that third large cognac, but somehow, she could not resist it, as thinking too clearly of her daughter's future wedding was a worse option. "Come, let me walk you home, Alexis. Everything looks better in the morning."

Alexis never arrived home, instead she was helped upstairs by Sir Arthur, who held a sobbing Alexis in his strong arms for most of the night.

Sir Judge Arthur rang Lucy a little late the following day hoping to catch her on her lunch break, but doubted she stopped for lunch, so when Lucy answered, it kind of caught him by surprise. He had not thought his conversation out, which was certainly not normally the case, and he blamed it on the late night.

"Sorry, Lucy, to interrupt your busy schedule but your mother has cried on my shoulder the best part of the night. Can you explain the situation?"

"Yes, I am to be married in a few days' time to Samuel. I wish it could all take place as Sally and Johnny's wedding did, but this is very different circumstance." Lucy gulped a tear back and muttered, "I am sorry to hurt my mother, and everyone, and so is Samuel, as he has family too, but this is how it is, and we don't want to wait."

"I do understand, Lucy, love is sometimes much stronger when we are young, why wait until the magic or worldly cares take over the love and romance." There was a pause and then, as if Sir Arthur had decided, he continued sounding much calmer and stronger, "I will speak to your mother and explain it the best way I can, perhaps that she is not losing her daughter but gaining a very talented son-in-law, leave it with me, Lucy, what day have you decided on?”

“Friday, at the loveliest restaurant, it’s got a strange name, owner’s son Anwar is organizing our wedding, so hopefully all goes to plan.” Lucy paused, then quickly spoke as she remembered something important, “Oh, I nearly forgot, I am studying to be a vet specializing in larger animals, horses, donkeys.” Lucy giggled nervously, thanked Sir Arthur, who she knew to be her father, and said her goodbyes.

Lucy sat on a large rock just outside the gate of the donkey sanctuary, when Eugene walked toward the gate and called out. “Hi Lucy, are you reluctant to enter and face the day? I am heading home as Sandals, the new donkey, has thrown his weight around all night.”

“Oh, poor Sandals, I love that little donkey, he is normally so good, whatever is wrong with him?”

“He is fine now, but I was working on my own and needed someone to hold him steady, poor beast had a thorn in his hoof, right on the tender part, he relented to the pain and lay down for me.”

“Clever Sandals, I wish you had rung me, Eugene. I would have come straight here, I was in bed early.”

Eugene raised his eyebrows and flashed his dark eyes at Lucy. “Lucy, my dear, I believe you have far more to think of and sort out at the moment. You must be excited.”

“I am very excited. In fact, I can hardly wait, and also I am worried!”

"Why on earth are you worried? He is handsome and clever, he is a remarkable young man, with lots of ambition." Eugene laughed and added, "You could do a lot worse!"

"I hardly know him, or at least hardly know anything about him, where he has lived, his parents, does he like coleslaw and pease-pudding party sandwiches?" They both laughed and left each other at the gate, Eugene to find the nearest coffee house and Lucy to commence her day in the sanctuary.

Lucy entered the dress shop and waited while a large box containing a wedding dress, headdress, and gloves for her wedding was opened. Penny, the shop assistant who had been given the job of showing Lucy the wedding dress, was so excited, which added to Lucy's joy.

"Look at the straps. Oh goodness, this is some dress." Penny gasps. "Let's look at the price first. This is going to be too expensive, I am sure."

"Come try it on, let's see it may not even fit you, although I am betting it will."

Lucy could not take her eyes off the dress and quickly turned to see the back in the large floor-to-ceiling mirror. The front of the dress hung from thin straps covered in diamonds and pearls, then gently caressed her breasts before clinging to Lucy's slender waist and hips. Lucy stood on her tiptoes as the dress spread out onto the floor. The dress was backless, held only by similar diamond straps across her back.

"Do not worry about the price, you can rent the dress." Lucy could not believe her eyes as she looked at her reflection, and now could hardly believe her ears.

"Thank you, Penny, yes, yes, please." Lucy knew she had the right pair of shoes to wear that would lift the dress the few inches it needed, so no expensive alterations or new shoes were needed.

Friday arrived and so did Sir Arthur and Lucy's mother. "How can you live in such dreadful conditions, Lucy. Have you forgotten your standards?"

"Oh, mother, give me a hug."

Alexis threw her arms tightly around her pretty daughter, who appeared to look even more beautiful than when she left home. Alexis liked everything done to perfection, but things here were very different, far more laid back. Anwar rang early morning, leaving a message.

"Lucy's wedding is planned for 12 noon. Can you and your guests arrive at the main entrance at 11.55 am? I am to be Doctor Samuel's best man, so I will collect him at 11 am and hide him in our private rooms until you arrive. All you have to do, Lucy, is get a taxi here. Ring if any of my messages are not clear, see you at your wedding. You will hear your wedding music playing as you enter."

"Goodness, Lucy, ring the man back he never said what room."

"No mother, we or at least I will follow the music."

Sir Arthur laughed at his daughter, who had the same tenacity as himself.

Lucy was helped out of the taxi by Sir Arthur, and Lucy asked the long-awaited question. "Father, will you give me away?"

"That is both sad and a pleasure, my dear girl." Alexis followed Sir Arthur and her daughter, and wished she had drunk the whiskey offered her.

As they entered the room where the music came from. Lucy gasped as there was Sally and Johnny near the front of the room. Samuel was on the other side of the room. There were no relatives on his side, only Eugene stood behind Samuel. Samuel turned to look toward his future wife and decided if any person could look as beautiful as Lucy, he would believe not only in fairies but angels.

Anwar grinned at Lucy, knowing she was delighted with his wedding arrangements. Flowers and miniature trees were everywhere and a large arch with white lilies draped through the trellis led Lucy and Samuel to where they kneeled. The priest was black African and wore an ivory long garment, incense was wafted around the room by two young men also dressed in ivory gowns, that swung the incense containers from side to side.

As the music stopped, the priest spoke loud and clear, and the service commenced. Samuel spoke of his love and said what had just come into his mind. "If anyone can look so beautiful as my darling Lucy can, then I believe in angels, for I am sure I have found one."

Lucy looked at Samuel. "Love has no age or time, and no wings, and yet it flies into our hearts when least expected."

"It is not to be fought with, only nourished, until eventually our roots will become one, and we will blossom."

Alexis sobbed, as she knew her daughter was so very right. Seize the moment, Lucy darling, as do any of us know what regrets we may have in the future.

Chapter 13
Unspoken Words

Alexis wanted to scream at all the years of happiness with Sir Arthur she had missed. She was wise enough to realize it was Lucy's declaration of her love for Samuel that had brought about her despair. After all, perhaps Sir Arthur would not have wanted her, only Lucy, his daughter. She decided to relax, have a drink and enjoy the moment.

As Anwar approached with a tray of champagne, Alexis' mood changed into positive. Sir Arthur was a very busy man it would never have worked, but now he was right here, and she decided to seize the moment. She smiled at her own foolish romantic thoughts. Sir Arthur held Alexis' hand and gave it a loving squeeze before leaving to find Anwar.

Anwar was hard to find as he rushed around seeing to Lucy and Samuel's needs. Sir Arthur did manage to catch up with him just as he was about to head into the kitchen. "Excuse me, Anwar, can I have a quick word please?"

"Yes certainly, Sir, I do hope I have not displeased you in any way." Anwar looked genuinely worried.

"No, not at all. Anwar. I am just asking for the wedding bill. If you have managed to print it out yet, no need to itemize it, Anwar, just give me a bill for the total amount, please."

Anwar was wanting to ask him to wait but then thought better of it, as he had gathered, the happy couple had no thought of the bill, neither had they even asked for an approximate quote. Anwar delivered a white envelope containing an invoice showing the standard amount, and a 30 percent deduction for goodwill. Sir Arthur disappeared once again and returned with the invoice and check for the full amount. He had also given Anwar a well-deserved tip.

Sir Arthur stood at the bar with Alexis waiting for the wedding lunch to be served. It smelled so delicious and he was starting to feel very hungry. From getting off the plane, he had not felt at all relaxed as the airport was very empty, and lots of flights had been canceled due to the virus. He decided to give a quick call to his secretary in England for her to check their flights.

He was not at all surprised with the results, all flights leaving tomorrow were doubtful, and the best option was to leave at 11.00 tonight. His secretary was also seeing to the ticket change for the 11 PM flight. He spotted Sally, who was congratulating Lucy, and headed over to explain the situation.

Lucy was so disappointed to hear they were leaving so soon, but when Sir Arthur suggested they stay at the airport hotel for two nights, Lucy felt a lot better as she had never given any thought to their honeymoon; in fact, she had given no practical thought to anything about the wedding, and yet it had all gone to plan perfectly.

Sir Arthur had booked two of the best rooms for Alexis and himself, so the hotel quickly changed one night to two and two bedrooms to one. The champagne and flowers plus dinners were to surprise Lucy and Samuel. The best thank you Sir Arthur received from Lucy was when Anwar came to sit them down at their wedding table, and Anwar said, Lucy, you are a very lucky girl not only to have found Samuel but to have someone like Sir Arthur looking after you and your mother.

Lucy replied without hesitation, "Anwar, he is my daddy and I love him."

The spicy traditional meal was delicious, and still in a full flowing wedding gown, and just a small vanity case containing nightwear and cosmetics, they all headed off to the Airport Hotel. Anwar had carried out his job to the letter and a white wedding car arrived with ribbons and bows.

Lucy smiled, thinking she was now a married lady to Doctor Samuel Sheridan. Samuel, reading her mind, pulled her close and kissed her passionately on the lips.

As Lucy and Samuel left, Anwar was almost in tears, he was normally a man of few words, but this had broken his silence it was magical. As these two young, and now married people who were not only devoted to each other but very special friends. He knew they would return to see him very soon, but as they left, a light seemed to go out. He shook himself down and finished a glass of champagne with total satisfaction.

The Airport Hotel took several photographs of the happy couple for their monthly magazine. Once again, the champagne flowed. Sir Arthur was far more relaxed, as he knew catching the earlier flight was more than sensible. He had expected that he would have had to seek a lot out for the hurried wedding; instead, he had been treated as a guest at his daughter's wedding. He had never felt so close to Lucy, his daughter and Alexis, who seemed to cling to his arm for support as she accepted her daughter's marriage.

Alexis and Lucy left the two men to go and refresh themselves. Johnny and Sally had taken themselves off to view the incredible displays of expensive garments in the shops of the hotel. Once alone, Alexis asked Lucy if she had any regrets. "No mother, not one. Why should I have? He is clever and handsome, and he loves me, and I certainly love him."

"What if he has to go away to work in another country, and there was no need to go with him, as there was no donkey sanctuary housing retired and injured donkeys?"

"Oh mother, please stop all these 'what ifs', I am married and happy to be Samuel's wife, please be happy for me, you will be leaving soon." Lucy's voice broke and she sobbed in her mother's arms. "I would love to be your little girl again, safe in my pink bedroom, but I trust Samuel will also make me feel safe. If not mother, you have my permission to sort him out."

Alexis giggled through tears and hugged her daughter. "It's just I feel I am losing you too soon."

Alexis and Lucy descended the grand staircase of the hotel and sat at a highly polished carved round table set for the six of them. Sir Arthur arrived at the table with a menu for the evening meal and Samuel was at the entrance of the hotel taking a call on his mobile. He arrived at the table with a smile on his face and told Lucy it was his dearest friend Lenardo wishing them happiness and congratulations.

Lucy wished they were not going to stay at the Airport Hotel after Sir Arthur and her mother plus Sally and Johnny leave, as it somehow gave her a sinking feeling. "We will be alright, darling Lucy, if we feel lonely, we leave and return to my apartment, or where ever makes you happy."

"We will enjoy this evening and see how we feel." Lucy squeezed her husband's hand in endearment and wondered how he knew exactly what she was thinking.

The dinner was delicious and the waiters all evening smiled at the happy couple, they then suggested they all make their way to the hotel foyer ready for the taxis to take them from the hotel to the Airport ready to book for their earlier flight. "It is best to leave now, Sir, said a very anxious waiter, who feared the flight would be quickly filled. The news is making people panic and leave early."

Sir Arthur leaped to his feet and quickly finished his whiskey and thanking the waiter and saying his goodbyes to Lucy and Samuel at the same time, fled with Alexis on his arm followed by a running Sally and Johnny to the waiting taxis.

Lucy felt relieved they had left in a hurry, as she had dreaded the final farewells. Samuel took Lucy to a quieter part of the hotel where they could have a drink and watch the plane take off. They were never sure if they had seen the plane Sir Arthur and Alexis were on take-off, but that was good enough for them, and they left hurriedly to return to their room and commence their long-awaited honeymoon.

The room was so pretty in ivory satin drapes and bed throws, the walls pink and satin wallpaper displaying wedding bells and storks.

The night was magical and the morning almost felt like it had arrived too early. When the same waiter who had served them at dinner tapped on their room door and entered, carrying a tray of every type of cooked breakfast from traditional to fresh spiced salmon, Lucy felt she was about to burst with happiness.

Samuel was handed a morning newspaper with the headlines confirming no planes were allowed to enter or leave the airport; he breathed a sigh of relief, and the waiter confirmed that Sir Arthur and Alexis had left safely with no hitch.

After a walk around the grounds of the hotel hand in hand and brunch at 11 AM of mushroom soup and scrambled eggs served with a green salad, the couple decided to take a swim in the pool on the top floor of the hotel and then get ready to leave. They did return to their room with full intentions of leaving, but after the tired couple lay on the bed for a quick nap, the next they knew it was 8 in the evening.

They had been awoken by the telephone and their familiar waiter asking them to confirm 9 PM for their evening meal. They were both glad they had stayed the extra night and were grateful for the long-needed sleep.

Lucy wore a cream silk sweater and white tight stretch trousers, the outfit was complete with gold high heels. Samuel complimented Lucy, wearing a cream suit and cream shirt with gold threaded through the fabric of the jacket. Neither was hungry and after a few drinks and a light snack, returned to their room.

Samuel rolled over in bed to face Lucy and whispered. "I love you, Mrs. Sheridan."

There were no words necessary from Lucy as she welcomed Samuel, her husband, into her open arms.

Chapter 14
Silence Is Golden

Lucy had such a lot on her mind, and so did Samuel, problem was who was going to be first to break the silence.

The happy couple had been back at work for nearly two months. Lucy felt homesick and ready to return to her roots. She missed her mother and Sally. In fact, she missed everything she knew as home. Suddenly her life felt very different from what she knew and loved, as if there was a huge hole, that was making each day feel empty and sad.

She sat in the sanctuary talking to Eugene, "I love Samuel so very much, but I feel lonely and lost at what I can change, it would be unfair to Samuel, who really enjoys his work here, and his life."

"Give it time, Lucy, sounds as if you need to write down what it is you miss as you are working with donkeys here just the same, also learning more and studying, you do not have to love it, just relax and do your best, as all will change."

Lucy felt better for Eugene knowing, somehow it was a comfort. Eugene brought up the subject of him driving a lorry full of donkeys to Brown's Donkey Sanctuary in the next few weeks. This made Lucy feel so much closer and far more connected to her home.

Samuel had a lot on his mind that he was not sure he would ever be able to talk freely about to anyone. He was a professional doctor, yet he had seen fairies. He never brought the subject up to Lucy as then he was making it very real, and that was the opposite of what he wanted to do. He wanted an explanation and lay awake most nights for hours, just thinking and wondering about his own sanity. Was he going mad or was it the start of his brain playing tricks on him?

He adored Lucy and found more each day to love about her. She was so easy to live with, just right for the man he was. So lovable, and caring, and yet she held back her future desires and put his dreams first. He knew Lucy would willingly return home, and yet he was not ready to return, after all, that was Lucy's roots and friends and although he knew a few doctors and medics from the hospital there, it was still not his roots.

In fact, Samuel was more inclined to travel and work for a few years in a few different countries. Samuel decided to wait a few more months and see what changes may have occurred.

Lucy could not believe she had been married to Samuel for six months. Each day she felt blessed, never regretting their early marriage to each other. She had made Samuel's apartment their home. Pretty colorful throws hung over a bamboo screen in their bedroom, that had a wicker rocking chair and bedrest to match. Colorful rugs lay over the tiled floor and a mirror door sliding wardrobe contained both their neatly hung clothes.

The lounge was still quite bare, a bureau and desk took the whole of one wall and were used by both most days. The kitchen was small, a breakfast bar with two stools was adequate for morning coffee and cereal but not much else. So, the couple ate their takeaway meals out or in their lounge. The white-tiled wet room was clinical and complete with a reliable shower, which was more than adequate.

They visited Anwar at least once a week and their friendship grew and filled the empty lonely hole Lucy had. Anwar had many relatives and each one was introduced to them. Anwar loved to tell the story of the romantic couple who walked up toward his restaurant so much in love, and how he arranged their marriage and became the best man. The story almost hypnotized the listeners, but always ended with laughter and smiles.

Eugene carried out his promise and delivered two dozen lame and old donkeys plus a very tired and old pony, to Brown's Donkey Sanctuary. Sally and Johnny were delighted as this helped Mr. Hill to remain at home and carry out essential work on the fields and barns relating to the donkeys. Sir Arthur insisted that Eugene stay in his home and rest up before making his journey back.

Sally managed to give names to the donkeys that had just arrived and after placing some old and new straw and patchwork bonnets on them took photographs of them. She placed them in various parts of the field before taking the photographs, some with other donkeys in the distance and some with outhouses and barns behind them. Their names were quite exotic and a little spiritual.

The naughty donkey that kept taking the other donkeys' treats was named Judas. The delightful two girls that appeared to love posing were called Alpha and Omega. Two others that looked like twins and loved each other beyond doubt were named Romeo and Juliet and Sally's favorite the little shy pony was called Sasha, and the others already had names.

Sally quickly had a rather nice little write-up about each one placed beside the photograph and by the end of the day already had people wanting to adopt most of them. Sally sang happily, knowing that some of the donkeys already had money coming in each month to help feed and pay for the vet's bills.

Johnny was back on his ship, so she quickly sent an email to give him the good news. She was just about to leave the office and return to the donkeys when the phone rang. It was Lucy who sounded extremely happy with her married life, but Sally definitely detected something not quite right. "What is it, Lucy? You can tell me anything as I can you, and we both know if we choose it will not go any further."

There was a pause as if Lucy was thinking about what exactly to say, whether or not to say how she felt or just fluff over it. She decided on the latter and gave a little laugh before replying. "Sally, forgive me for I am just being silly, I think I just miss you all, especially you."

"Oh, Lucy, and I you too, it's dreadfully lonely here without you, even when Johnny is home, it's like a light has gone out."

"Soon I will be home I pray, even if it's just for a week or two, it's coming up to almost a year, and Samuel has no intentions of returning, quite the opposite he is now talking of work in Majorca. Which is great but the Spanish know more than I about donkeys and horses, it's in their blood, plus I want to further my qualifications and still intend my studies to be a vet."

Sally knew she would have to end the call as she had to get to the donkeys. "Lucy, I need to go and attend to the donkeys which have multiplied recently, so please do not think badly of me, I do believe Majorca is a wonderful island, also only takes a few hours by plane to visit home, did you not take a course in Spanish or was that German."

"Thank you, Sally, I never thought how easy it would be to visit home and yes, I took a brief course in Spanish, I would need to refresh and work out what sort of job to apply for."

Sally giggled, then replied, "You could always ask the fairies."

Lucy did not go straight home, nor did she return to the sanctuary after her call to Sally, instead she walked down a very narrow street she had seen often but never ventured. It looked so interesting, with flags draped at regular intervals across the street. A lady arranging some garments on a rail outside her shop smiled and asked if she would like to enter and have a browse. Lucy smiled into the lady's warm brown eyes and pointed to a white linen blouse she was hanging up.

"I am sure it would fit you, and the price has just been reduced."

"Yes, thank you, I will take it."

Lucy continued on her journey down the street, clutching her a cream carrier bag containing her new purchase. Yet something did not feel right, and she had no idea what. A wine bar on the end of the street, its large oak arched door across the corner, making it appear more like a church than a bar.

Lucy entered the dark bar and as her eyes adapted to the darkness, she could see apart from a group of young men in the corner and a couple sat at the bar, it was empty. Lucy made her way to the bar and sat on a high-backed stool. She quickly sent a text to Samuel, who she knew was taking a half day off, and one to Eugene explaining the situation. She then rang Eugene and explained a little better than she had in the text.

"Eugene, I need to think, as I love Samuel but something is missing and I really do not understand what it is, I am in a bar at the end of Flag Street, I am fine just need this space and time to think, I will be in work tomorrow morning prompt."

Lucy did a lot of thinking and very little drinking, which disappointed a new young barman, who wanted to impress his boss, who was sitting outside in the shade.

As Samuel entered the bar, Lucy almost fell off her stool with surprise and delight. "My darling, what is wrong? You can tell me anything, I went to the sanctuary and Eugene greeted me with the information of my sad little wife." Samuel put his arms tightly around Lucy and, forgetting the other people in the bar, kissed Lucy as if there was no tomorrow. "I am never letting you go, Lucy. You are my wife and my life."

"I love you, darling Samuel, so very much but something is missing, and it makes me feel empty, but what it is I have yet to discover."

"Then Lucy, my love, let us ask the fairies."

Chapter 15
Ask the Fairies

Lucy wished she could see Horace and Horace 2nd, but truthfully, she so wished to see the fairies. She pondered on how she could contact them and wondered could it be the fact she was now living with Samuel in his apartment.

Somehow that made sense to her, and so she decided to spend the night alone in her old room, which was still empty. She asked Samuel but already knew that Samuel would never object as they were now one and only wanted each other's happiness. "Of course, my darling, come let me drive you over after you finish your meal."

Lucy lay on top of the colorful throw on her bed and smiled as she looked around the small familiar room. She felt happy and a feeling of warmth seemed to circle the room, knowing she would soon be seeing the fairies. She somehow just knew she would and felt she could cry with happiness.

Fairy Snowbell and two Miss Daisy Weed flower fairies flew in from the small opening in the window. They were all smiling at Lucy and Lucy returned their smile as her eyes drifted over them. Lucy spoke first, "I have so missed you all, at times I thought I was quite mad and that I had imagined it all, but here you are sitting on my bed. I have never felt so happy, never."

"Lucy, we are always here for you but now you are not alone, you have Samuel, who loves you and donkeys that so need you."

"Yes, I agree as I have asked myself that also many times, what is it with me that appears to have so much, and yet at times feels I have not much at all other than an empty, lonely space that is not fulfilled yet."

"Lucy, what makes you is the love that you give so freely to the donkeys and spiders, especially our special spider Horace, you live in that lovely peaceful, and loving world, and without it, you lose your reasoning to your very existence."

Lucy lay quiet thinking; how what Snowbell had said made total sense. She did not want to step too far into that huge world. She had experienced such cruelty and sadness, she craved for her cozy slippers and pink dressing gown and a feeling of warmth knowing she had helped the donkeys in Brown's Sanctuary and could feel safe and secure sitting in her bedroom reading up on donkeys' illnesses and spiders cycle of life.

Suddenly, everything was uncertain. Lucy explained to the fairies. "Please understand I just miss the feeling of familiarity, I will work hard here and wherever Samuel takes me with his work, but I have lost myself."

"Or maybe you feel you have lost your inner peace, your soul perhaps." Snowbell coughed and sneezed gently into a pretty maple leaf. "You have not lost yourself at all, you needed to 'spread your wings'," Snowbell stopped and giggled, showing a peaceful fairy expression across her incredible face.

"I don't want to spread my wings any further, thank you. This is as far as I wish to go."

"Oh Lucy, you have only just begun, and Samuel is so strong, go with him to Myjorca, and then let us talk again. In the meantime, try to write about all the fairies in Mr. Hill's garden, by doing this and telling the stories of the adventures we have shown you so far you will feel your inner peace returning. Be strong, Lucy, you do not have to change yourself because you are in another country, close your eyes, Lucy, you can be anywhere you wish, just use that powerful imagination you have."

Lucy woke hearing a Cockrell singing his wake-up call, as the sun danced across the small bedroom. She could not remember the three fairies leaving but she could most certainly remember and understand what they had said. Life felt so good, and Lucy quickly showered and dressed, ready for work in her denim overalls.

First, she would try to catch Samuel before he left for work and tell him how much she loved him. She also knew if she was not with him, she would not be complete and then no way could her love and imagination flow into a children's book. I *believe in fairies,* she thought, *and I am happy that I do.*

Samuel was delighted to see Lucy. "I have missed you, darling. Please do not make a habit of leaving me, even if it is to see the fairies."

They both laughed and kissed each other as if they had been separated for far longer than a night. "Do you think me a little crazy believing in fairies, Samuel?"

"I too, Lucy, had a very strange experience that involved a fairy; in life Lucy many things cannot be explained, we only know little and we leave the rest in our open mind, and why not my dear believe in lovely pretty fairies, who only want to help, I am proud they are your friends, what a privilege to carry through life."

"Samuel, fairy Snowbell wants me to write about all the fairies and I cannot wait to pick up my pencil where I left off, I will do illustrations also and tell stories about my many experiences."

"I am so proud of you, darling Lucy, let's get all you need, and perhaps you can make a start tonight."

Lucy almost danced to the donkey sanctuary, she had her inner peace back, the inner peace that passes all understanding.

Chapter 16
Elfvil and Cecil Transporters

"What are you doing with those baby rabbits?"

Elfvil ignored the question from the flower fairies and walked swiftly away down a burrow that Cecil had just begun to run down. The frightened baby rabbits followed, although some hid behind rocks that were in the burrow.

"Elfvil, stop please, they are so afraid, they're only babies!"

Elfvil's reply was short and said hastily. "They fit!"

"What fits where, Elfvil?"

"The little rabbits fit."

The two Miss Daisy Weed flower fairies decided Elfvil was in no way going to enlighten them, and so they decided to follow and see for themselves. As they half ran and half flew along the burrow, a roar of an engine was heard coming toward them. The two flower fairies lay flat against the wall of the burrow.

What sped toward them appeared to be a train, larger than a child's train and made the sound of a mainline express train. It was so loud it was deafening, and the baby rabbits ran everywhere to escape the train and the noise. The train stopped and Elfvil climbed down from the driver's seat, he was wearing an inspector's cap and held a red flag.

"Can you two Miss Daisy Weed flower fairies help put these little rabbits that appear to be all over the train lines, into the carriages, as we are training them to make many different train journeys."

At that, Cecil stepped down from the first carriage, he was wearing a station master's jacket with silver buttons and a matching black cap. "Clear the line immediately, I am late; in fact, we are all late, how late I say, yes say how late, remains to be seen, yes seen, er, remains to be, yes."

"Cecil, what on earth are you doing, and late for what?"

"For what, for what you ask, do I have to be late for, er what, er something, I am neither late for what or something, for I am just late!"

Elfvil grinned at the flower fairies and asked them in a very authorized voice. "Would you like to get on board now, as I fear we may run you over?"

"Where will you take us and the baby rabbits, Elfvil?"

"As far as your eyes can see."

"What sort of answer is that Elfvil?"

"I feel quite pleased and satisfied with my answer. Now quickly help get these rabbits onto the train as we are now running late."

The flower fairies had no idea why they did what Elfvil asked, and no sooner had the last baby rabbit been placed in the last carriage of the train, than the engine roared at full power, and the train shot along the line. The problem was, the burrow was far too small in diameter to cater for a miniature train of this size. The powerful engine of the train fought against the walls of the burrow until eventually, it gave up. Elfvil had not given up thou, as he screamed for Cecil to get his very largest and strongest rabbits to dig them out.

Poor Cecil hated failures and asked could Elfvil find them a bus or even a few cars. Elfvil agreed to everything, he felt more powerful than the engine, and so needed. He decided it was not his clever master plan to transport rabbits around the many burrows, nor was it the train's fault, it was the fault of the rabbits that were too lazy to make larger burrows.

"Oh, Elfvil, how could you say such a thing, burrows were not made to put train lines in and run trains, besides where did you find the train, it is rather dashing!"

Elfvil was delighted that the flower fairies liked his new toy. "When I found it, well Cecil found it and I put the lines together as best I could, as some were missing, we do not know where it has come from, it just appeared to drop through the top of the burrow a little distance from here, we also found some golf balls and a bag containing golf clubs, oh and a sign which we intend to use saying Miniature train to Crazy golf, did I do good little flower fairies and will Manszard be pleased with me, as I was afraid to return to the black tower last night as I am not sure, maybe I have done bad."

Elfvil hung his head and genuinely looked confused. "I do believe you have done exceptional this time, so top of the good list, why do you not return as soon as possible to the black tower, and explain to Manszard what has happened, also Manszard may be able to help with extra lines, and larger burrows."

No sooner had they suggested this to Elfvil than he was gone in a puff of green smoke. The little rabbits were now even more terrified and so Princess Precious was called to bring their mothers and take them home. Fortunately, there was enough space on either side of the train to get the mothers onto the train to collect the sobbing baby rabbits. Cecil was walking up and down the carriages with Elfvil's red flag explaining the situation to no listeners.

"Everyone, I say everyone, to depart from the train as quickly as possible, yes, possible as we appear to have hit a landslide, a burrow side, nuts, and a leaf to be given to all passengers of Elfvil and Cecil's transport, we hope you have enjoyed, yes enjoyed your journey, and look forward yes look forward with interest, er yes interest to your return journey."

Cecil sat in an armchair watching a log on the fire burning, Princess Precious sat in a similar but smaller armchair, she smiled proudly at her husband, and he smiled back with satisfaction. "I will need you to wake me early, yes early I say, as I have another busy working day."

Precious jumped to her feet and shuffled away to prepare a packed lunch for her clever busy husband.

The two flower fairies arrived back at Fairy Glen late as they had been given the task of sorting out which baby rabbit belonged to which mother. There were dozens of baby rabbits left on the train with no mother collecting them.

They were more than sure some were Herbert's wife Willameaner who frequently forgot about her babies and that the rest were probably Princess Precious, who was totally confused with the part of responsibility, believing that having them was enough.

Herbert arrived and sniffed over the rabbits, and then shyly admitted there appeared to be less children in his burrow and that he would take the ones that smelled of oil, as some of his youngsters had been oiling the train. The two Daisy flower fairies, which were now extremely tired, placed the remaining rabbits on their wands and flew at speed along the burrow to where a little arched door with Mr. & Mrs. Cecil was. They tapped a few times and eventually a very sleepy Cecil opened the wood door.

"Yes, I say yes, what have you here are they to stay the night, er, the night I say."

"We believe, Cecil, they may be your children."

"Oh very well, you had better, yes better I say, say bring them in."

Princess Precious returned from the kitchen and spied the baby rabbits sitting in front of her, their wide tired eyes staring in amazement at her, and the room they stood in, that they had never ever seen before. Princess Precious looked down at the three rocking baby cradles placed in front of the fire that were empty, then looked down at her large tummy. Precious was almost sure but not certain, had she had her babies and forgotten, or was she about to have them?

It was all too difficult to remember, so she quickly took two baby rabbits in each arm and placed them in the cradles, there were two rabbits left with no cradle, so she popped them behind the cushion on her chair, to sort out later. Cecil got up from his chair to take the flower fairies to the door.

"Good night and safe, yes, safe journey, oh er, and thank you, I think, yes, I think."

Cecil scratched his head and returned to his fireside chair. He glanced around the room at the baby rabbits that stared back at him, the babies had all decided to keep quiet about their past as this was a very glamorous burrow.

Chapter 17
I Am Telling You the Truth

Cecil looked earnestly at Princess Precious and calmly repeated, "I am telling you the truth. She is a baby rabbit, our baby rabbit."

Princess Precious tried to read her husband's eyes, which looked very honest. "I tell you, Cecil, that is a hare. Look at her long legs, and huge ears, she is a hare, and I have never given birth to a hare, even if it does have a white bobbed tail!"

"I am keeping her, yes keeping her and her name is Hetty, yes Hetty." Princess Precious sat nibbling a carrot left over from her breakfast and giggled. "Hetty, the hare, she is a hare, ask her."

"I will not be so rude, yes rude, ours, all ours."

Princess Precious laughed out loud and almost choked on her carrot, she knew exactly why suddenly this overgrown rabbit, which was definitely a hare was so important to Cecil.

The hare was not very old and had been left behind when Monsieur Albert had arrived at the hairdressing saloon with a dozen of baby hares for grooming. She was a very inquisitive hare and had wanted to see around these historic burrows, she had discovered the train and thought she would have a little nap in the driver's seat.

She had fallen asleep and was discovered by Elfvil, who carried her on his wand into the passenger carriage where many rabbits huddled together. She was not sure how she had arrived at Princess Precious and Cecil's home, but no way was she going to jeopardize such luxury. The hare stood up straight on her hind legs and walked slowly toward Cecil and sat at his feet.

"Oh, now can you see the resemblance, yes resemblance?" Cecil smiled showing all his teeth, some teeth with pieces of broccoli stuck in between, and carrot chewed but not swallowed, lay at either side of his back teeth.

The hare followed her new owner and smiled her best smile, showing a selection of green vegetables stuck in between most of her long teeth. Princess Precious had never enjoyed such entertainment in a long time and giggled uncontrollably.

"Yes and yes, dear husband, now I see the resemblance, for you are like a mirror image of each other when you smile."

Cecil was so excited. "She is ours, well mine, all mine to help me, and clean and carry for, er me, yes, me."

Hetty, the hare, rushed to the slipper box at the side of the fire and placed a pink pair of fluffy slippers on the cold paws of Princess Precious, who laughed more and more as her paws were tickled with the fluffy slippers. Cecil sat with his paws on a purple pouf, waiting for his slippers to be placed on his tired paws.

Hetty cuddled and hugged her wonderful new father and placed the gray fluffy slippers on his paws. Princess Precious was happy as her husband rarely relaxed, yet somehow this rather adorable hare had calmed not only her husband but all in the burrow.

Hetty did eventually contact the Hare Union as she knew she was being exploited, it was when Cecil asked Hetty to clock in and out of her working day. At first, Hetty did not understand, but Cecil enjoyed explaining it so he could see if she was wasting any time. Hetty could not believe her ears and defended herself, as she reminded Cecil she was not being paid.

"Oh, then as you were, yes were, Princess Precious and I were looking after you as we would our daughter, yes daughter."

Hetty sobbed I don't want to be your daughter, you are wearing me out, look at my claws, they are worn right down, and I have lost many kilos in weight while you and your wife are getting fatter and fatter as you sit all day, ordering me to fetch and carry.

Hetty, however, did not want to leave Cecil or Princess Precious as she loved them both, she just wanted a bit of kindness and compassion, and so she continued sobbing through the night and the following day, until Cecil totally gave in to her. "Yes, and I say yes, all is granted you may sit all day and I and my dear wife will do everything, yes I say everything, besides I will lose my incredibly good looks if I sit any longer in front of the fire."

Cecil had been told by the Daisy flower fairies that he should not make these rabbits work for him, and that he should be grateful for them just being there, but Cecil found that very hard to understand. He was a business rabbit and too old to change his ways. *He decided to be kind to Hetty, but only for a short time, then he would get her to clean the burrows, yes, all the burrows,* Cecil thought.

The Daisy flower fairies arrived a few days after the incident. They sat with Cecil and explained how Hetty had been left on the train, and most importantly that she was a hare, not a rabbit. This Cecil ignored, Hetty, in Cecil's mind, was his daughter and that was that.

He also knew Hetty would settle, as she was loved by all his family, and love conquered all. He believed Hetty was stronger than she was, as she was very tall, with large ears and long legs. He now could see the error of his ways, she was a loving, warm, and a friendly hare that needed love and a good home.

Cecil looked into the faces of the flower fairies, "I love her, yes, love her, as my daughter, she is free to go whenever she wants, but please, please dear flower fairies do not take her away."

There was a long pause, then Cecil continued, "In fact, yes, in fact, we all love Hetty."

At that, all the rabbits who were listening stood up on their hind paws and clapped Hetty. Hetty stayed a long time with her adopted parents, but did eventually marry a hare who she met one sunny morning while gathering acorns. It was love at first sight, and Big Ears, a very fine hare, understood the love she had for her adopted parents and set up their home close to the burrow she had lived in most of her life.

Cecil and Princess Precious visited Hetty and Big Ears every day and most nights. After all, it was their daughter.

Chapter 18
Lucy, Where Are You?

Lucy held tight to three baby rabbits that had been placed on her knee. She could barely move and when the train sped along the line, she felt she would be suffocated with the amount of diesel fumes and rabbit hair which blew everywhere. Two of the rabbits wriggled and Lucy could feel them slipping off her knee.

"Hold on, I will drop you." The third rabbit hopped off her knee and squeezed into a small gap between several other baby rabbits. Lucy could not quite make out where she was apart from on a train with hundreds of baby rabbits.

"Where are we going?" she asked but no one answered her question. "Were you going to bed, and who, yes who, are you?"

The baby rabbit asking the question did not wait for an answer as it ran off to where five baby rabbits sat in the corner of the carriage eating a large carrot between them. "Why would I be going to bed? Am I not making a train journey in a rather small carriage, with all these baby o rabbits," Lucy asked. "I am a hare, not a rabbit!"

"Then perhaps you would be so kind as to inform me where we are all going."

"Maybe you do not know where we are going. Is it a surprise?"

A little beige and white rabbit with a pink nose decided to answer the question. "Yes, yes, that is it a surprise, we are going to get a surprise, yes surprise, are you sleeping?"

"Why would I be sleeping?"

At that, Lucy stopped and stared into the face of a little green elf, who she had seen briefly before. "I recognize you, who are you and what are you doing with all these baby rabbits, oh and hares, and also me?"

Elfvil felt extremely important and smiled with a knowing and very annoying grin. "We are going on a train journey!"

"I realize that, but why and where to, please you have to tell me as my husband will be worried."

"I am just a lovable elf with half a sin completely gone from me, and do not have an answer as I believe you are dreaming and intruding in our pleasure time on the Oriental Burrow Train." Elfvil paused a little too long, and his audience began to scratch and snore. "I suggest you wake up before the next stop as we need to re-fuel and pick up more passengers. You are too big and take up all our pre-booked passenger seats."

Lucy knew this was reality, not a dream, she was definitely on a train with two baby rabbits sitting on her knee, she looked down to confirm her thoughts, and was totally shocked to see she was wearing her pink nighty. "I want to go home now please, who has kidnapped me, please let me go, let me go—" Lucy trailed off but struggled to be free, as Samuel held Lucy tight in his arms.

"Lucy, wake up darling, you are safe."

Lucy opened her eyes wide and stared, not knowing who this man was that was holding her so tight and calling her name. She decided to sleep and escape all this confusion, she was quickly back with the rabbits, and she rushed along the train feeling she was flying rather than running, and looked for the baby rabbits.

"They have all gone. All our passengers are now at their destination, we now need to clean the train. Please go home now."

"Who are you and where are the baby rabbits, and where is my home?"

"Rabbits are home safe, and you live with I believe someone, yes someone." Cecil was more than pleased with his clever reply and now wanted desperately to return to his dear wife, Princess Precious.

Cecil hurried along the train line and Lucy decided to follow. The tunnel was a lot bigger than a burrow and Lucy found it easy to follow Cecil. *Suddenly, Lucy had lost Cecil, he must have turned off somewhere,* she thought, and spotted several small doors on the left of the tunnel. She knocked on each door, but no rabbit answered.

She tried pushing the doors and each door was unlocked leading to a burrow. She rushed down the first burrow wishing she was home, but where, where was her home? *She could hear a beautiful sound she did not recognize, what instrument makes such a wonderful sound* she thought.

She pushed open a small door on the right of her and was more than surprised by what she saw. It was Cecil, the same rabbit she had been following, he was stood Infront of a white rabbit that was standing upright on a wooden rocking chair, and she was singing.

"You must go immediately, no more trains tonight and now I have to help my wife, yes my wife Princess Precious, with her singing lesson."

"She is quite incredible," Lucy said with a smile, "I have never heard such a wonderful sound. Can I please listen?"

"No, no, and no I say, you must go besides we are going to have supper then go to bed, you must, yes must go."

Lucy woke and smiled at Samuel. "I believe I was dreaming of rabbits on a train."

Samuel turned over and smiled at Lucy, "Was there a white one?"

"Yes, Samuel, there was, and she was singing!"

"Coffee, darling?" Samuel had decided not to pursue the rabbit venture and smiled to himself. He decided that being married to Lucy; he would never get bored. Less than an hour later he was driving Lucy to her donkey sanctuary, Samuel could not take his eyes off his wife as she looked so fresh, showing no signs of lack of sleep or nightmare.

Lucy, however, did feel troubled as the nightmare she knew was real, and that it would not be long before she saw the rabbits or Daisy flower fairies again.

It had been a very busy day at the donkey sanctuary, and when Lucy arrived home, she felt relieved that they were just having a quiet night in. Samuel had arrived home early and was busy in the kitchen cooking a pasta dish. He turned around as Lucy entered the newly painted kitchen with the cream walls and pale clover kitchen doors, the colors she had chosen against Samuel's suggestions of white walls and black kitchen doors.

He placed the lid on the pasta pan and reached out to his pretty wife, who he had thought about all day, despite the busy wards which were still quite full of patients suffering the aftermath of the deadly virus. "How are you, dear wife?"

"I am well, just a little tired and hope we are having an early night!"

Samuel kissed Lucy and made his eyes dance at the mention of an early night. Lucy gave Samuel a knowing little tap on his hand and they both laughed. "Of course, darling, an early night we both deserve. Let's eat and maybe a glass of wine or two and then bed."

Samuel was asleep and Lucy gently lifted his arm, which was wrapped around her and lay it at his side. She quietly wriggled away from him and lay on her side, a little afraid of the sleep that awaited her that she fought against.

"Lucy, you have to come with us now, please Lucy."

Lucy opened her eyes fearing who was there, two little Daisy flower fairies with smiling faces looked into Lucy's wide eyes. Lucy did not answer and could feel the cold air as she flew with the Daisy flower fairies to her familiar home.

"Is it my mother? Is she ill?" There was no reply. "Is it Horace, is he?" Lucy never finished her sentence; she knew house spiders rarely lived longer than six years.

"No, not Horace, although he is very old and now can barely walk also his eyesight is failing, but no not Horace who misses you so very much, it is Queen Bee, and only you can help."

Queen Bee stared back at Lucy and tried to walk toward her with her wings down by her side, but she staggered and fell, lying on her side. "Oh, how sad! What can I do to help Queen Bee?"

"Lucy, Queen Bee is dying and wants to be taken to where she went with her parents as a child, it is a wonderful place a long way from here in the grounds of a large castle, it is her last wish."

Lucy tried to recall the life of bees and could not understand the reason for wanting to die away from her loyal subjects. The flower fairies reading Lucy's mind answered her question. "Queen Bee has served all her subjects and also her own family and has shown the world of Bee's dedication, she is now old and dying and she wants to go to where she flew free, playing Bee games with other young bees."

The Daisy flower fairies spoke in unison. "She needs to be placed in something comfortable and then she asks you to take her to her place of rest, will you do this, Lucy, she has only been out of her confinement two times, once when her home was destroyed and another time when her son took her to the fairies party."

It appeared a long distance, but Lucy could not imagine how they appeared to be there instantly. Lucy held a toy bed taken from her doll's house in her old bedroom, which had not changed at all. Queen Bee lay under a small pink patterned doll's blanket, her head nodding.

Lucy carried Queen Bee carefully and placed the toy bed down carefully on a windowsill in the old stables where her happy memories were. Playing horse games, teasing the horses as she flew without fear under the legs of the tired horses. How she laughed when the stable boys rushed in to see why the horses were crying out as they feared a sting.

Queen Bee laughed as she would never have stung them, she was still laughing when she lifted her head from the small white pillow Lucy had placed for her comfort. Lucy knew she was saying thank you, and she replied by using her little finger to stroke the head of this tired Queen that had given her all. Queen Bee took her last breath, content she had done her very best and now would meet the creator of all.

"How were the rabbits, darling?"

"No, not rabbits, Samuel. Queen Bee, she was dying."

"Lucy, is she dead? Bees are so clever; I am glad you helped her!"

Samuel decided to leave the subject of singing rabbits and a dying Queen Bee, he kissed his wife goodbye and drove to work feeling incredibly happy, what a wonderful world I live in as I do believe it's the land of the fairies!

Chapter 19
Lucy Clairvoyant

Two Miss Daisy Flower fairies sat quietly on Lucy's bed; they had waited patiently for Samuel to leave for the hospital. Lucy woke and reached for the glass of grape juice placed on her bedside table by Samuel, she was just about to smile with the endearing thoughts she had for her thoughtful husband when she spotted the smiling flower fairies.

"Why are you here, you are like Horace, everywhere I go, well maybe not but I do appear to see you in my dreams or nightmares, what are they do you know?" Lucy stared at the flower fairies and waited for their reply.

"Well, you are in dreamland, asleep but what you see is real or a premonition!"

"So, what does that make me, apart from very strange."

The flower fairies smiled and spoke together, "Very clever," they paused, then added, "also very useful."

"This is no answer I need to know what is going on, as I fear I may be going crazy." Lucy stopped abruptly and sat upright in bed, her face in a state of panic. "Samuel, Samuel,

I have to get to him, there is going to be a dreadful accident, the children we must find Samuel."

Samuel was just about to get out of his car in the hospital car park when he noticed his phone vibrating. "Yes, Lucy, are you alright, darling?"

"Samuel, do not go into the hospital get the children out of their wards."

"Why, Lucy, you have to explain more. Have you had a nightmare?"

Samuel never finished the conversation instead he watched with horror as a large delivery wagon carrying oil drove into the entrance of the hospital. Lucy could hear screams and cries for help but heard no sound from Samuel.

She screamed through the phone repeating his name and then pulling her work trousers and a jumper which she had carefully left out the night before, and quickly left in her jeep for Samuel's hospital. Arriving Lucy could see flames the height of the three-story hospital building, and screams so loud, Lucy knew would haunt her for a lifetime, feeling confused for a second about what to do.

She decided to drive around the back of the hospital as the hospital was built on a hill. Lucy could see nurses and children at windows, of the second floor, so she drove as close as she could and then beckoned the nurse to open the window and make a bedsheet rope, it was then she spotted Samuel at another window where he waved her over to.

One by one a child was lowered down to where Lucy stood with her arms outstretched to catch the terrified sick child. Lucy placed five small children inside the jeep and began placing others in the trailer she used for transporting her sick or lame animals. When there was no space left, she lay them lined up on the grass verge.

The heat was intense, but fire engines seemed to be everywhere and rumor spread fast that the fire was now under control. Ambulances arrived close to where Lucy had placed the stunned children and each child was taken to a nearby hospital that had been opened and used for the pandemic. Lucy held a very subdued Samuel who shook uncontrollably.

"You're safe, my darling. Samuel, you are safe."

Samuel collapsed his body hitting the tiled floor of the back entrance of the hospital. An ambulance driver shrieked to a halt as frantic Lucy waved her arms for help, he ran to Samuel, and at the same time, a young student doctor rushed to help. Lucy stood in shock as she watched her husband being rushed away in the ambulance.

She drove the jeep with care, her hands shaking as she followed the ambulance. She parked the jeep in the car park of a private hospital less than a mile from the hospital Samuel worked in, and where such a tragedy had taken place.

Samuel was carried on a stretcher to a private ward, Lucy quickly followed and waited in the corridor until the doctor examining Samuel gave her the OK to come in. "He is badly shaken, and his right arm is badly burned, fortunately, it's minor burns but nevertheless, we need to keep an eye on them, you must be his wife."

Lucy felt embarrassed and yet proud to be Samuel's wife. "We will keep him in the hospital tonight and examine him in the morning to see what is best to do." The doctor was about to leave when he turned and asked, "How did you know to warn your husband?"

Lucy thought for a while and then faced the doctor with her honest eyes and replied. "In truth, I just knew, although I was not sure what exactly had to happen."

Samuel tried to sit up in bed to interrupt any further questioning. "You see I have a very clever wife, her mind and gifts would fascinate the cleverest professor, however, Lucy can neither explain nor understand these gifts, there are many things that we cannot explain, and the incident at the hospital and my wife's warning is one of them."

Although the doctor had left the room, Lucy knew this was not the end of questions. She knew that this doctor who she believed to be Egyptian had lost a child and he would want peace from Lucy in some way. How Lucy knew she did not know she just knew.

Lucy stayed by Samuel's side until he fell into a deep sleep, and then made her way to the entrance doors, she was exhausted and wanted to run a hot bath and have a glass of wine, to melt the horrors of the day away. As she was about to step onto the stairs of the hospital leading outside, she heard her name being called.

Lucy knew before she turned around who it was the doctor who had just attended her husband was rushing toward her. "Please, can you help me, can we go for a coffee somewhere, I promise I will not take much of your time?"

Lucy knew it would be the opposite as this was not about Lucy but about his daughter.

"I want to ask you something."

Lucy stared back at the sad dark eyes of the doctor. "Yes, I know it was your daughter, oh, and a swimming pool."

"Yes, but how do you know? Come, please let's go in here." The doctor led Lucy into a rather nice hotel almost next door to the hospital, and into a small tearoom, with a lot of very well-dressed ladies who sat with their partners. Lucy sat down and the doctor ordered coffee and toasted teacake.

"I believe your daughter had flu and you asked her to remain in her bedroom while you had visitors to your home, in Egypt I think, your daughter quietly crept downstairs and made her way to the swimming pool, she was only young about seven or eight and she loved swimming."

"She could not stop coughing and she began to heave as she gasped for air she was confused, lack of oxygen you see, she thought the bottom of the pool was the top, so as she struggled, she began to drown, I also believe she was never a strong child!"

The doctor stared at Lucy and explained his daughter was almost eight, he never knew exactly till this day what had happened to his precious daughter. "I am Egyptian and that happened in Egypt, where my wife lives, you see she has never recovered from the shock and believes our daughter our only child was murdered, as she would never go against our wishes, why would she leave her room?"

"She did call out to you 'Daddy', several times, but someone had music on in the kitchen, so she came downstairs hoping to see her mother or father, as she was thirsty, and not feeling at all well."

Lucy felt so sad telling the doctor all she could see in her mind's eye. "I am sorry, forgive me, I need to return home, the hospital may ring me and besides I am quite exhausted it has been a long day and rather frightening, I nearly lost my husband, please excuse me."

Lucy almost ran from the doctor who desperately wanted her to stay and give more and more detail. He had no time to answer Lucy so he decided to follow her to her jeep. He called out to Lucy as she was just about to get into her jeep.

"No, no, please leave me alone!" Lucy escaped the doctor's cries of sorry and drove home.

Lucy entered her kitchen opened the fridge and poured a very large glass of cheap red wine that seemed to taste better if chilled, Samuel had placed the wine in the fridge almost a week ago saying we cannot drink that it's dreadful, corner shop wicker basket job lot. Lucy gulped the wine and refilled the glass, not caring of the quality, the bouquet fragrance was far from her mind and taste buds.

After a long bath, Lucy was beginning to comprehend what had happened. She lay back against the padded pink headboard of the bed and cried. "Do not cry, little Lucy, all is well because of you!"

Lucy opened her eyes in disbelief, yet not fearing. "What now, little flower fairies? What on earth is to happen now?" Lucy sighed and began to cry louder.

"You are clairvoyant, someone who sees clearer the future."

Lucy looked directly at the Daisy flower fairies, with a look in her eyes that was accusing them of all these weird, unexplained happenings. "Lucy, we needed your help as we could not have stopped this incident ourselves, how could we, please do not cry, surely you can see how without your help people would have died, children mostly and your husband."

Lucy gulped and reached for the glass of wine that sat on her bedside table half drunk. "Yes, I can clearly see that, but what now, is my life doomed with people wanting to know some message from their departed loved one, or how to dodge a disaster."

"You are right, Lucy, as you have a gift, not given by the fairies, it was yours from birth and you can use this gift as you feel fitting, it is yours, no one else can control it, use it correctly, you will learn everyone at some stage in their life needs help, to continue being who they are."

The fairies sat quietly for a while, their pedals looked dry, and their stems had brown dried marks on them. Lucy placed a glass of water beside the tired fairies and although the water had stood on the bedside table since the day before the fairies welcomed the water and splashed it over each other.

Lucy thought how kind and caring they were, never thinking of themselves and happy with warm water a little stale. Lucy cried more and spoke more honestly to the fairies. "I always knew I was psychic as long as I can remember, mother also knew I was."

Lucy could recall the teacher reading the morning register and asking did anyone know why Heather is not in school today. Lucy remembered telling the teacher she had fallen over the banister in her home. It was a little time later that Heather's mother arrived to tell the teacher the story of her daughter falling over the banister.

"How did you know Lucy?" asked the teacher and Heather's mother, the question was never answered. Lucy always ate chocolate to block these unexplained things that became many over time. Many schoolchildren avoided Lucy and called her a witch. In later years, she was welcomed in their company as they saw her as special.

Samuel returned home a few days later. He had a bad cough caused by smoke inhalation and both his arms were bandaged where he had been burned. Samuel and Lucy did not talk about any part of the incident, although Samuel tried to make a joke by suggesting the fairies may treat his badly burned arms.

He regretted his joke, which fell on stony ground as Lucy avoided his eyes and left the room. Samuel found Lucy outside the front door, sitting on the step. "Come now, darling, we are both alive and the children are all safe. Let's not query or talk but rejoice about it."

It was a relief to Lucy as to what good was talking about the situation and events. In the following days leading to the weekend, however, a lot of red wine was consumed by both, in silence, as they digested what had taken place.

It was Friday morning when Samuel suggested they got a cheap flight back to the United Kingdom, Lucy could hardly wait, she searched the internet and found one-way cheap tickets and then made her way to the donkey sanctuary to let them know she was taking her holidays. They were busy, so Lucy did feel bad about leaving so suddenly but she knew that both Samuel and herself needed this break desperately, as they were both exhausted before the incident and now needed to rest and recover.

They were leaving for home early in the morning Lucy had sent emails to her mother and Sally, and a more informative email was sent to her father Judge Arthur, who had replied immediately and offered to be at the airport to drive them home.

Lucy knew Judge Arthur would have explained the situation briefly to Sally and her mother. Johnny was home on leave and checked all their houses were stocked up with plenty of food and refreshments. His grandmother was also informed, and she set to making her famous brown bread and strawberry jam.

Lucy had slept a good few hours on the flight, but it was as if a delayed shock had happened as she vomited what seemed like every hour and cried bitterly. "Lucy darling, we are safe do not be sad, we will recover at home and I, for one, cannot wait to see familiar faces!"

Lucy wondered how Sally would greet her and wondered what memories it would bring back for her. It was not so long ago that Johnny was fighting for his life after contracting a virus on board his ship while Sally and he were on honeymoon. Lucy remembered clearly waiting for their return and wondered would this be similar, although in reverse, Sally and Johnny waiting for her and Samuel. Lucy was woken by Samuel as the plane was about to land. "Darling, we are home!"

It was dark when they landed yet Lucy spotted her father in his cream jacket looking out of a window in the airport directly at her, as she came down the stairs of the plane, and stepped onto the tarmac.

Judge Arthur hugged his daughter tightly and after collecting their suitcases, drove them slowly home stopping occasionally for Lucy who looked as bad as she felt. "It could be delayed shock, it was a terrifying experience for both of us, it's impossible to get the frightened children at the windows of the hospital out of our minds. Samuel gasped and took a deep breath to compose himself, If Lucy had not stopped me."

Samuel could not continue and kissed Lucy's hand as she trembled with the memory.

Lucy was greeted at the door of Mr. Hill's house by Sally, who threw her arms around the sobbing Lucy, who gave in to her built-up tears. Samuel was greeted by Mr. Hill, Johnny, and a very excited Sally, who had waited patiently for the call from Sir Judge Arthur to say he was heading home with Lucy and Samuel.

Johnny and Sally had disappeared into the kitchen to make cheese and pickle sandwiches, also egg and tomato in the delicious brown bread their grandmother had made for Lucy and Samuel's return.

Lucy was so grateful for the hot tea; she ate little but managed to keep the food down for the first time in days. Samuel noticed and assured Lucy that her sickness most definitely was due to shock. Lucy smiled but was really not so sure.

Come, Lucy, let's go upstairs and sit on my old bed and confess all. Sally took Lucy's hand and led her to her old bedroom which was now used as a spare room, Sally now used her older sister's room which was much larger, almost twice the size of her small room, and very bright. Mr. Hill had kept the two rooms his older daughters used to have, exactly how they had left them, just in case they returned home. Now all rooms had been changed and the small room that Sally had was about to be changed!

"Spill, Lucy, tell all, why are you looking so pale, was it that dreadful fire at the hospital, why on earth did the tanker, was it a tanker, drive into the entrance of a hospital?"

Lucy sobbed, "I saw it before it happened. What does that make me?"

"Lucy, it makes you a very gifted and a special person, you are clairvoyant, someone who sees the future clearer than most, and my dear friend, I always knew you were, well since you helped with the donkeys."

Lucy nodded as she did agree to have knowledge of what was wrong with a donkey before the vet examined the donkey, especially when she concentrated, where it came from, she was never sure.

"As long as the gift you have is always used to help, then it's a wonderful gift, although I would imagine quite draining."

Sally was beaming with happiness and could not wait to tell Lucy her news. "Lucy, look I am having a baby."

Sally pulled her long pink fluffy jumper up to display a rather protruding tummy. "I am only 4 months and just cannot wait to see my baby, please Lucy tell me you are pleased for me."

"Sally, I am delighted, why wait, you and Johnny will be a complete family, it's wonderful news."

Sally continued in a more serious way, "Lucy, we never ever took precautions, it somehow never seemed right for us, so when after all these months I was not pregnant, we were beginning to think something may be wrong with one of us."

Sally waited for Lucy to speak but then explained, "When I thought I may be pregnant, I could not believe it and tested and tested. I am so happy I fear I will burst!"

Lucy giggled and patted Sally's tummy gently, "I also fear you may burst."

The two girls were just about to return to their husbands and fathers when Lucy stopped dead in her tracks and stared at Sally. "Oh Sally, no no, I can't be, can I."

Sally rushed off and returned holding a pregnancy test. "Best you know, for it appears to be something we cannot hide for long, and maybe as Samuel has said, your sickness is due to the shock of the dreadful incident, where you, Lucy, my dear friend, was a hero."

Ten minutes later, Lucy sat holding Sally's hand while they kept their eyes glued to the test result. Lucy jumped up from the bed as the test result showed she was pregnant. "We never ever talked about babies, we never even spoke about the future, we more lived in the moment, I am not sure that Samuel may feel it's too soon."

"Stay here, I will ask Samuel to come upstairs to you that way you can tell him now and find out, if he is not happy by our lovely Lucy giving him an heir then you have all of us who will be delighted." Sally left and Lucy picked up the test and smiled. "Well, I never saw that coming."

"Never saw what coming, Lucy?" Samuel asked as he entered the bedroom. Lucy handed Samuel the test result. Samuel still not realizing what Lucy was trying to tell him. "Yes, I know Sally is pregnant. Johnny has just told me the wonderful news, I am so happy for them and Lucy we need also to talk about when we want our babies."

"I believe Samuel that is not a decision we can make as I already am pregnant, that is my pregnancy test, not Sally's." Samuel did not answer and just sat down on the bed, feeling quite numb with the news. "Oh, Samuel, are you displeased with the news? I never planned it."

"No darling, I am happy beyond words, but wonder what sort of doctor I am that I did not know his wife was pregnant." Samuel held the sobbing Lucy, as she repeated, over and over. "Our love baby."

"Yes, darling, and the fairies did not tell you that."

Chapter 20
Magical Moments

It had been a magical night as they celebrated their future babies. Judge Arthur called and was greeted by Mr. Hill with the wonderful news. "Come in, my friend, you and I are going to be grandparents."

A shaken Judge Arthur and a smiling Mr. Hill made their way to the whiskey decanter.

"Allow me, Sir." It was Samuel who could not wait to share the news, nor could he wait to be offered a whiskey to calm his nerves. "Tell me Sir Arthur, are you pleased with the news of your future grandchild?" Samuel asked with a shaking voice as he poured three large glasses of whiskey.

"I am shocked and delighted at the same time and you, Samuel, are you pleased?"

"Oh yes sir, more than I can express and still shaking from the shock, as I also have just found out."

Samuel sunk into the large red velvet Victorian armchair and Sir Arthur bent over him and placed his hand endearingly on his shoulder the two men beamed at each other. They wiped their happy tears away, laughed, and drank their whiskey.

"Come, let's go into the drawing room where Sally and Johnny appear to have a little more good news, I have filled the brandy decanter as I fear we need a brandy for the shock we have all had, and goodness knows what we are going to hear now."

Sally and Johnny waited until all were sat comfortably down and a drink in their hands. Sally smiled warmly at Johnny, who then took center stage.

"Mr. Hill, as you know, your daughter was asked to make an appointment with her doctor today she had previously been to the hospital to see a gynecologist." Mr. Hill sat down and sipped his brandy. Johnny realizing he was taken too long over the news and worrying Mr. Hill decided to cut directly to the news. "No, Sir, do not worry, this is wonderful news. Sally is having twins!"

"Oh my! Oh my goodness! Oh my, Sally, my darling girl, what delightful news." No more words came out of Mr. Hills' mouth, he just sat staring ahead, quietly drinking his brandy.

Lucy and Sally spent a little time in Sally's old bedroom looking at albums of the donkeys and talking about plans for improving the sanctuary. They talked about how they would manage once the babies arrived. The girls knew each other's strength and had no doubt they would manage.

The men sat discussing their plans, Judge Arthur pointing out that he would shortly be retiring and therefore he could be more hands-on, but Johnny and Mr. Hill reassured him they were happier with his academic input to the sanctuary, Judge Arthur felt quite relieved and remembered his attempt to replace some fallen fence.

Lucy's mother arrived a little later and hearing the news, she spoke her concerns. "She should have spoken to me first; she is too young and she will never cope. Why she never dressed her dolls correctly, always back to front, wrong shoes, then the poor doll was dropped somewhere." Everyone laughed.

Horace 2nd laughed too as he quickly made a speedy getaway out of an open kitchen window, which was just about to be closed to keep the cold night frost out. Horace 2nd headed straight to Fairy Glen to tell the flower fairies. He had turned more and more like his father, and after his grandmother died, he tried to take over where his father had left off.

Horace was weak now and extremely frail and although relied on his son for news still managed to crawl on a good day to see the Daisy flower fairies.

Horace 2nd found his father busy mending or attempting to repair his web. "Father, I have interesting news about Lucy."

"Then tell me all as I am worried I have not seen her, and I know she has just returned home."

"Yes, father and she is having a doll that she will not dress correctly and drop it."

"Are you sure you have this right, how will she have a doll, she must be lonely, so is her mother getting the new doll, as unfortunately it is true, you see she gets bored, I had a web, a very good web across the face of her last doll. It was so comfortable, I used to curl up on the eyes of the doll, the eyelashes were so soft, but Lucy never knew, she had thrown it in the shed one day, just before she started to cry."

Horace 2nd was just about to crawl away then remembered a little more, "Oh, everyone is having a baby or two."

Horace waited until his son had left, then made his way to where he knew the Daisy flower fairies would be. He was pleased with his son but doubted he had heard correctly as everyone having a baby or two seemed hard to believe, did everyone literally mean everyone.

Horace scratched his head and tried in vain to put all the thoughts of all those babies out of his mind, where on earth would they keep them, surely not in the barn. Horace spotted the flower fairies lying side by side in an old fox glove that had some special fairy dust to make it last through winter. "Wake up, little flower fairies, I have some important news you will want to hear."

"Go away, Horace, we need to sleep." Horace picked up a small twig that had broken off its apple tree in a bad storm and decided to poke the flower fairies. "Don't be so rude Horace!"

"Rude Horace rude, I think not, I think rude cloned Daisy flower fairies, telling helpful kind old Horace to go away."

"OK, spill, Horace."

"Still rude, how you have become so coarse, it must be your traveling. Perhaps you have learned your bad grammar from the rabbits."

"We are sorry, Horace, and you are quite right, we have no right to be so rude to you as you are our dear and wonderful friend." Horace began to cry and told the flower fairies his news, in between blowing his nose and drying his eyes. "So, you see, everyone is having one or two babies, except Lucy who is having a doll."

Horace turned and started to crawl away, delighted at how the flower fairies had described him. They called after Horace in unison, "Horace, would you like us to see what we can find out as perhaps we are missing something, we are very interested, and thank you for this valuable information, which we will also inform our elders about."

A little while later, after Mr. Hill and Judge Arthur had discussed the situation of the girls out loud, sitting on the seat in the wildflower garden. The flower fairies decided Horace 2nd, needed to be taken with a pinch of salt.

However, the news had taken their breath away, and quickly informed the elders of the girls' conditions. The elders were delighted and explained that babies were loved by all fairies, unbeknown to their mothers, fairies comfort babies when they cry. No one could quite fit the doll in unless it was for a baby girl. The good news was Lucy appeared to be home for a good while.

The Daisy flower fairies remembered their own buds and pined inwardly for them. Their choice to work and help others on the planet had come with a price tag.

Lucy sat quietly on her mother's bed thinking of where her life had gone or was going. She had given up quite a bit helping the donkeys and also being a good wife to Samuel and now going to be a mother. What am I doing, she asked herself. Her mobile had two messages, one from Sally and one from Samuel. She read Sally's first.

"Hey Lucy, can you look at Shane's right hoof just looking up the field with my binoculars and he appears to be limping badly, that's the new brown small donkey with the platted tail, came from a traveling theater group, thank you, Lucy, so glad you are home."

Lucy smiled and replied, "Yes, Sally, and I will give out carrots also, and great to be home, see you later."

She read Samuel's text and replied, I love you, with a kiss. Somehow or somewhere, all her doubts had gone, and she felt she had never been happier. That is life, Lucy, if you're kind and help others you may be tired but you will certainly know great happiness. They were her mother's words ringing in her head.

Donkeys were all fed with sticks of carrots and Shane's right hoof bathed after a stone was removed, a small white bandage was placed gently around the ankle to please a very funny donkey who skipped off down the field toward his friends delighted with his bandage.

Lucy was so happy to be home. It felt so right and when Samuel returned from his interview with Doctor Bernstein, she knew all was right with the world. Samuel chatted freely about how well his interview had gone and explained he would be starting work at his old hospitals' children's ward.

"I can tell the children who have little hope and dreams of a future with the fairies."

Chapter 21
Two Prams a Funeral
and a Wedding

Two cream and silver prams sat side by side at the front door of Mr. Hills' cottage. June and July had been wonderful months. Sally had given birth to two wonderful healthy babies; Johnathan, the image of his father and Ruby, the image of her mother and named after Sally's deceased grandmother.

A few weeks later, after the birth of the twins, Lucy gave birth to Daisy, a very striking baby girl that appeared to want to entertain anyone who cared to look into her pram. Mr. Hill opened the oak door to check on the two girls, he was carrying a small bundle wrapped in a pale blue blanket, and he placed his grandson in the pram next to his granddaughter.

He walked back inside his home and sat in his favorite armchair. Judge Arthur called through the open door to Mr. Hill, not hearing a reply, he made his way into the lounge where he spotted his friend sitting. At first, he thought Mr. Hill was sleeping, but something did not seem right, and he quickly rang 999.

"Yes, Sir, it's my friend Mr. Hill. I think he may have had a heart attack, please can you come quickly, I cannot find a pulse."

Mr. Hill was declared dead on arrival at the hospital. Sir Arthur thought how it was less than an hour since they had pushed the babies in their prams around the village, like two very proud grandparents. There was no consoling Sally who lay on her father's bed sobbing, Lucy tried in vain to get Sally to open the door, it was hours before Sally came downstairs to feed and change her babies.

Johnny was back at work and so Judge Arthur sent a telegram to his ship marked urgent. Lucy's mother Alexis was wonderful, and Lucy wondered how she knew such wonderful words to calm Sally. "I can be your mother! Would you like that, my dear? I can be there for you as I am for Lucy, and I do love you already as my own."

Sally nodded and clung to Alexis while Lucy held her hand. Johnny telephoned to say he was able to leave the ship at the next port and would be home within 48hrs. Lucy changed all the babies and handed her baby Johnathan to feed. Ruby lay quietly, waiting her turn. Lucy then fed Daisy and gave way to her grief.

Sir Arthur had heard Alexis' sincere words to Sally and walked over to Alexis, who appeared to be shaking. What if I die, what about my Lucy who will be there for her, Sir Arthur placed his arms around Alexis. Alexis buried her wet face into his chest and was not sure what he was saying. She withdrew from his arms and held back in order to hear his whispered words.

"Marry me, Lexi Lou. Marry me please. I love you and we can both be there for the girls and their babies and the sanctuary. I have wanted to ask you to marry me for such a long time. Will you darling at least think about it, I have lost my best friend I don't want to wait until I lose you to someone or I die, life you have to grab, what do you say?"

"Yes, yes." Sir Arthur sat quietly down, taking in Alexis' yes.

The girls were told of Sir Arthur and Alexis' engagement to be married a month after the funeral of Mr. Hill. Mr. Hill had left a lot of instructions to Sir Arthur as he knew his days on the earth were drawing to an end, he said he felt tired and yet so happy with everything, especially the babies, and asked Sir Arthur to step in and take his place.

It appeared to all who heard the Will read out that Mr. Hill could see Sir Arthur and Alexis married, he asked them both in a very endearing letter that left no one without tears, "Look after my darling Sally."

Sir Arthur had walls knocked through three cottages after his marriage to Alexis, and the three cottages supplied three very happy couples with space which was certainly needed as the families grew. The cottages had been one home originally so a part of history had been repeated but never before had the sound of so many children's happy laughter fill the rooms of those cottages.

The Daisy flower fairies flew many times to look into the prams of the crying babies. They wondered why Sally had two babies and poor Lucy only one, then they thought of the rabbits with all their large families. Perhaps they both should have had more.

Elfvil sat on a toadstool with an envelope in his hands. It was addressed to Miss Daisy Weed's flower fairies and contained a handwritten note from Markszard inviting them to the black tower for refreshments tomorrow morning. They always felt nervous visiting the wizards but Markszard was not at all scary he was a gentle wizard not like Manszard whose wizardry would scare the bravest of fairies. "Will Manszard be there and if so, should we take anything?"

"Yes, as he has questions for you, not difficult ones, and please, can you bring me a fairy wand?" Elfvil grinned mischievously.

"Nice try, Elfvil, and no."

Fairy Snowbell, who had her back resting up against the toadstool that Elfvil sat on, decided to make her presence known. "The questions, Elfvil, are they about the sanctuary after the death of Mr. Hill?"

"Yes, fairy Snowbell, you are also invited."

They left early morning before the fairies in Fairy Glen began to wake. Snowbell flew in the middle of the two flower fairies. All three enjoyed flying through the sky together, just like old times. Both wizards greeted them on arrival, and they were taken to a cozy room high up in the tower.

The fire had just been lit and the warmth was so welcoming to their cold tired wings. It was always the very last part of the journey to the black tower, which was the most tiring as the tower kept moving away from them.

Markszard offered berries and slices of melons to the three fairies, Snowbell did not need to be asked twice and ate the berries without thought for the journey back. The Daisy flower fairies landed on a juicy slice of the melon where they drank some of the delicious juice. Manszard sat on a red velvet high-backed armchair to the right of the fire.

"I wish to ask you questions regarding any changes that will occur to the donkey sanctuary now that Mr. Hill is no longer with us, although I believe he is still close by."

Snowbell decided to answer Manszard first. "It is truly so sad and thank you, Manszard, for caring about the situation, Sally and Lucy intend to run the office work and see to the feeding of the donkeys which are many, with more arriving soon."

"Lucy, although qualified in many useful ways, is still not qualified as a veterinarian, she intends to enroll to continue her studies at an open university. So, they still require vets visiting most days. Johnny does as many repairs as he possibly can but there is little time spare when he comes home on leave due to their two babies, and old grandparents."

Manszard listened and stroked his long beard as he thought of what needed to be done. "Snowbell, you and the fairies are no doubt helping to keep those crying babies calm, Elfvil has been around Fairy Glen quite a lot just to hear and report back to me, and what also appears to desperately be in need of repairs, is the many fences that have blown down in the angry storm we had last week."

Markszard handed a notebook that contained drawings of which fences were needing repair or replacement. Manszard glanced at the page appropriately and continued, "Elfvil has repaired the roof of the barn where several tiles were missing, he has also taken Buster, Sir Arthur's dog back home after he found him outside his garden, as the gate has been badly damaged and will not close properly."

"I, Manszard, will see to all these repairs tonight one-minute past midnight, it is a full moon, and my energy is very high, then I, Manszard, will rest and perhaps my two daisy friends will come and visit me perhaps bringing me some well-deserved honey."

Snowbell flew across the room and faced Manszard, she was so close to his face that Manszard could feel the air beneath her wings, as she thanked him with all her heart.

"You are both so very quiet, little Daisy flower fairies, can you tell me what is troubling you. I have been watching you both closely, are you tired is that what is wrong?"

"Yes Manszard, that is exactly what is wrong. We are so very tired but do not want to be planted in the earth as we love having legs and wings."

Manszard looked so very sad, as this was certainly not what he expected to hear. "We also considered being pressed flowers and we both lay down on Lucy's open book, but that did not sound very pleasant to us, and we leaped up just in time before Lucy not only closed her book but then dropped it into her leather satchel which she uses to take her books back to the library, so goodness knows where we would have ended up."

Manszard laughed but the flower fairies did not instead they began to cry. "Tell us please what is to become of us, we really are tired and yet we love being Daisy flower fairies that travels around the world to help, we truly wish we could help more, it is just."

The Daisy flower fairies did not finish their sentence. "I will speak to your elders to see what is the best solution for you bot. In the meantime, rest and do not worry, oh, and stay away from open books."

Chapter 22
A White Feather

The three fairies sat on their upturned toadstools waiting for midnight, they could see Lucy and Sally holding their babies at the window as they watched the full moon move across the sky. Something felt mysterious and magical to them all, even Sir Arthur stood at a downstair window looking out, Johnny had checked the doors were locked something felt eerie to him.

Colors shot across the sky as midnight struck. Lucy knew something magical was about to take place that would affect them all in some way, especially the donkey sanctuary. She could hear the donkeys making unsettled noises, which they often made before a storm.

Lucy felt pleased that they were all staying close, Lucy and Samuel were staying at her mother's home, Sir Arthur and Alexis were going between all three cottages checking Sally and Johnny were safe and Lucy and Samuel, while Buster followed his master around and the babies were seen by all.

They had all decided they needed each other to be close, while they recovered from losing Mr. Hill. Sir Arthur felt relieved the sanctuary had been placed legally in Sally and Johnny's names, and he realized his dear friend, who he missed beyond words, had thought everything out thoroughly.

Sir Arthur watched a very magical night that he knew could never be explained and hoped Lucy had experienced it and viewed it from her window. Daisy had kept her awake, and Lucy stared in amazement at the sky. This Sir Arthur knew was something for Lucy's book, another unexplained incident.

The following day, Johnny sat at the breakfast table with a cup of coffee and a large brandy. He decided he must be going quite crazy and handed Sally his mobile. Look darling, can you explain this?

Sally was looking at picture after picture of the most incredible fences, high and secure around the sanctuary. Lucy answered the call from Sally as she sat feeding Daisy, hearing the wonderful news of the fences, she whispered quietly to her baby, "It's the fairies, Darling Daisy, it's just the fairies."

The flower fairies were also watching the display of colors in the night sky, the full moon lighting Fairy Glen. They could see two elders coming toward them in the moonlight, it was Snowbell and Tinkerbell, they were smiling and told the flower fairies to get ready for the flight of their lives.

They felt tired and wished they could just be left to sleep, and yet something inside them was telling them both they had to go. They flew a little higher than the black tower where Manszard and Markszard greeted the Daisy flower fairies. "We will take over the flight now and keep you informed."

The Daisy flower fairies were handed over to the wizards who took flight immediately after placing the flower fairies securely in their cloaks. Up and up, they appeared to be flying but where were they going both flower fairies asked each other as they sent telepathic messages to each other. Perhaps to the moon, and yet they felt they had passed that a long time ago.

They had both fallen asleep so did not know how long or far they had traveled. Manszard woke them both and placed one on Markszard's hand and the other on his, they then placed their other hand gently over them, protecting them from the brightest light. "This is the light of the world, we must follow it and then we will hand you over to very special angels who will look after you forever, the fairies have let you go because they love you both."

"Please Manszard, we will be good, let us stay with the fairies at Fairy Glen."

"You will still see the fairies and all who you love from time to time, but this is the solution, no soil with your roots in and certainly no flower fairies pressed in Lucy's library book, and no tiredness."

A bright path led up to a golden gate, and as they approached the gate began to open and two angels greeted the two flower fairies in total silence. Their faces glowed with happiness and the flower fairies loved these angels beyond words. As they followed the two angels, the golden gate closed tight, and the wizards could only look on with wonder.

Messages were sent to the elders at Fairy Glen, telling them all was completed and that the Flower fairies were now with the angels in heaven. The fairies had felt angel dust being sprinkled around Fairy Glen.

Lucy knew something more than magical had taken place, more spiritual she thought, *so when a white feather floated down from nowhere and landed on her pink writing book, she had no doubt and suspected it may have something to do with the two Miss Daisy Weed flower fairies.*

She picked up the white feather, opened the pink book, and began to read what she had written.

The Life and Times of Miss Daisy Weed.

THE END